THE FIRST MISSION

BOOK TWO OF THE SHADOW ORDER

MICHAEL ROBERTSON

Email: subscribers@michaelrobertson.co.uk

Edited by:

Terri King - http://terri-king.wix.com/editing
And
Pauline Nolet - http://www.paulinenolet.com

Cover Design by Dusty Crosley

Michael Robertson
© 2016 Michael Robertson

The First Mission is a work of fiction. The characters,
incidents, situations, and all dialogue are entirely a product of
the author's imagination, or are used fictitiously and are not
in any way representative of real people, places or things.

Any resemblance to persons living or dead is entirely
coincidental.

All rights reserved

MAILING LIST

Would you like to be notified of all my future releases and special offers? Join my spam-free mailing list for all of my updates at www.michaelrobertson.co.uk

CHAPTER 1

Seb battled for breath as he followed Sparks across the rocky and barren landscape. Life had been hectic since they'd signed on with the Shadow Order. In his line of work, he had to use his fists and now fought when he needed to—promise to his dad or not. It had been unrealistic to think it could have been any other way.

"There it is!" Sparks shouted.

Another glance behind and Seb saw a wall of laser fire coming straight for him. Everything slowed down as it always did when he sensed danger. It gave him time to telegraph the beams, twisting and turning in a complex and uncoordinated dance to avoid them.

One came so close it nearly took Seb's nose off and he went cross-eyed as he watched the blue beam shoot past him. He froze. A red blast ran near enough to snap him out of it and he ducked to avoid another shot that would have cut straight through his skull.

Although he'd seen Sparks point through a gap in the wall of red rock, Seb couldn't see what lay beyond it from his current position.

As Sparks vanished through the space, Seb gritted his teeth and found an extra burst of energy. Sweat ran into his eyes and his throat dried because of the hot environment.

Before Seb got to the path through the rock, another wave of fire came at him.

Seb ran backwards to see the blasts and his stomach lurched as he anticipated a fall on the uneven terrain.

At least forty indigenous creatures charged in their attempt to reclaim their queen's crown, which had already vanished with Sparks. Maybe male, female, or both, the quadrupeds were the size of lions and dressed like ninjas. Black cloth covered their entire form save for a cut-out slit exposing their yellow eyes and a hole so they could use their huge jaws. They were each armed with a blaster on a leather thong around their necks. It slowed them down to turn bipedal, but when they did, it allowed them to send another volley of fire at Seb.

The bars of red and blue laser blasts spewed forth in their third assault. Seb dodged all of them again, his ragged breaths slow as his world moved at a fraction of the real speed. Although he could see the creatures' weak spots, he ignored them. He'd lose if he stopped to fight.

Before the creatures could loose another round of fire, Seb came to the pathway through the rock and ducked into it. The planet's thin atmosphere made every breath less effective than the last.

The red terrain on the other side of the wall seemed redder than the side Seb left behind. The rocky landscape burned a deep crimson like fresh blood.

A space of about fifty metres separated Seb from the huge mountain Sparks headed for. Halfway there already, she ran for a large metal shutter embedded in the side of it. Their intel had told them they would find a hangar nearby and, so far, the information they'd received from the Shadow Order's databank had been spot on.

Before Seb followed Sparks across the open space, he stopped. Out of breath from the run and with the dry taste of dust in his throat, he forced his words out and called to the small Thrystian, "How long will you need, Sparks?"

Sparks spun around so she ran backwards and cupped her mouth to call to him, "Come through when you hear a ship's engines start up."

A deep breath to try to level himself out and Seb gave Sparks a thumbs-up before he turned back to the gap he'd just run through.

The first of the quadruped ninjas burst out and Seb ambushed it with a punch to the forehead. The thing didn't see it coming and its momentum carried it forward despite its head being snapped back by the blow. Out cold from the attack, the beast slid along the hard ground face first.

The next one came through and Seb kicked it in the same spot. It wouldn't be a challenge to knock them out one at a time, but he'd be overwhelmed if he tried to do it to all of them.

Hot from the run and the red planet's elevated temperature, Seb knocked three more out with quick jabs, each one connecting with the hard skulls of the beasts. The next deep breath he took smelled of wet dog. In fact, it reeked of it, and he ruffled his nose as he looked at the dirty unconscious aliens.

Seb opened and closed his stinging hand to try to ease the deep pain already in it. Too focused on his fist, he missed the next attacker, which jumped over both the bodies of its unconscious friends as well as Seb. Before he could deal with it, three more came through the gap.

Seb ran at the creature that had jumped him and knocked

it out. The beasts behind quickly caught up and surrounded him, their deep growls rumbling like race pod engines. Yellow eyes glared at him from their black masks and they snapped their wide mouths. Their lips pulled back to reveal their black needle teeth. Each bite could take his head clean off. Matted brown fur hung from their maws, clogged with what looked like congealed blood from their last kill.

One lurched forward and Seb kicked it under its jaw, careful to avoid puncturing his shoe on its sharp bite. It yelped and pulled back, but it stayed conscious. This couldn't last long; there were too many for him to fight.

A glance at the gap in the rocks and Seb saw more stalk through the space. They all watched him, their heads dipped low and their shoulders lifting on one side and then the other as they strode forward. Confident in their dominance over him, their rattling growl joined with the others around them.

Just one of the creatures stood between Seb and the hangar. He lunged at that one and drove a punch to its hard forehead. He could have sworn he heard his hand crack. Numbness spread through his fist, but he took off toward the mountain. Blaster fire hit the ground around him and sprayed him with chips of red rock.

Just a few metres clear of the group, Seb turned to see he hadn't made a dent in their numbers. They came through the crevice like a flood. What he'd thought to be forty of the brutes now looked like seventy or more. A plague of beasts rather than a pack. Although, they seemed less interested in using their blasters now.

Pinned between them and the mountain, Seb had no hope of distracting them until he heard an engine start up. Hopefully, Sparks had a plan B.

Every tired step against the hard and rocky ground snapped through Seb. Clumsy with exhaustion, he didn't have the strength in his body to compensate for the unforgiving surface. With sore hips from the run, a throbbing hand from the fight, and burning lungs because of the planet's thin atmosphere, he used the beasts' slathering and phlegmy rattle to spur him on.

As Seb closed down on Sparks, he saw the shutter in the side of the mountain lift by no more than thirty centimetres. Enough for her to get through, but it looked tiny for him.

When Seb looked behind him, the creatures had gained on him. The ones at the front remained on all fours while a row further back now stood on their hind legs as they released another round of laser fire.

Most of the shots went woefully wide, but one came so close to the tired Seb he only managed to avoid it at the last moment. A fizz and then the acrid reek of his singed hair snaked up his nostrils from the near miss. Were everything moving at full speed, he'd be dead a hundred times over by now.

Sparks had said to wait until he heard a ship's engines, but what did she expect Seb to do? Dance for them until she'd finished?

Before he'd reached the shutter embedded in the blood red mountain, Seb heard the *whoosh* of a booster. One thing about Sparks, she never let him down—apart from the time she'd robbed him.

With the partly raised shutter just metres away, Seb turned to see another wall of red and blue fire. He dropped to the ground and every shot flew over him. Metal sparks exploded from the shutter as a firework display while the lasers played a tattoo against the alloy barrier.

As Seb rolled along the ground, the beasts' stampede ran a heavy vibration through his back. The desire to turn and look at them fought for his attention, but he shuffled forward and slipped his left leg and foot into the hangar on the other side of the shutter.

The beasts continued their charge as a landslide of chaos. Seb slipped further into the hangar, but his chest and head trapped him. He turned his face to the side and looked at the oncoming rush of animal ninjas. Despite trying to pull his body through to safety, he remained stuck.

Seb pushed up with both hands against the cold metal shutter. He strained so hard his head spun and his tired lungs burned. He managed to lift it by another few centimetres, but he still couldn't get through.

The first of his pursuers caught up with Seb and stamped down on his right arm. Its huge, clawed paw—easily the size of Seb's head—pinned him to the hard ground and sent sharp pains through his bicep.

The rumble of the creature's rasping wheeze filled Seb's ears and he smelled blood on its hot breath.

Seb's eyes watered from the sharp sting on his shoulder blades as the rough ground tore him to shreds with his fight to get through. But with more beasts closing in, he had to keep going and tugged against the one that had him trapped.

The creature lifted its foot, tucked its opposable thumb in to make a fist, and drove it toward Seb's face. By taking the pressure off his arm, it freed him and gave him the chance for one last attempt to get away.

The ground shook from the creature's punch. A slowed-down vibration through the rock because of Seb's perception, the blow would have crushed his head had he not moved it.

Seb thought he'd gotten free until the beast pinned him again, this time getting his lower arm.

Like it had with Seb's bicep, a deep burn seared his forearm and it quickly turned numb beneath the heavy pressure. Blind to what was occurring on the other side of the shutter, he felt warm metal tap against his hand. The creature's blaster!

Despite being pinned down, Seb reached up with his right hand. He had enough movement in his wrist to catch the blaster and snap it from the leather thong around the monster's neck.

The weapon hit the ground and Seb saw it through the gap amongst the collection of paws on the other side. It lay just in reach. He moved quickly and rolled over to use his left hand to snatch the blaster, angled it up, and pulled the trigger in one fluid movement.

The creature who had him pinned screamed and ripped its large foot away.

Seb withdrew into the hangar just as the metal shutter shook with the collision of several large bodies.

CHAPTER 2

Unlike the dry and sparse planet, Seb found the hangar to be crammed with objects. Ships, tanks, buggies … The chrome on all of the vehicles glittered in the space as stars would in a night's sky, and the entire place reeked of engine grease. Strip lighting ran along the ceiling and stood in stark contrast to the dark red glow of the planet outside the hangar. It forced Seb to squint against the glare, his eyes stinging from the violent change in his surroundings.

The deep rumble of a ship's engine rolled around the space and Seb felt the vibration of it run through his feet. He scowled as he looked for which ship made the sound and finally saw a fighter on the other side of the hangar. Sparks sat in the cockpit. A quick scan of the gleaming ship and Seb saw she'd picked one large enough to make the jump to hyperspace, but small enough for a dogfight. Just the thought of a battle in space tightened his stomach and sank dread through him. The walkway to the ship lolled from the vessel like a metal tongue, and he ran for it with what little strength he had left in his aching body.

Once he'd halved the distance between him and the ship,

Seb saw Spark's tense face turn to horror in the cockpit. He looked behind to see the creatures who'd chased them were forcing the shutter higher and several had nearly shoved their way through.

Still armed with one of the creatures' large blasters, Seb held it with two hands and fired. Despite the shutter being big enough to cover a gap that would let a tank into the place, he missed it completely and hit the wall next to it. An explosion of red rock blew away from the impact and did little to slow the creatures down.

Seb fired again and this time he hit the shutter. As it had done on the outside when the creatures had shot at him, his blast exploded in a shower of sparks. Although a spittle of fire rained down on the beasts, it only made them flinch before they continued to force their way in. "Damn it," he said as he turned around and willed his tired body toward the ship.

With about five metres to go, Seb looked behind again to see four of the large creatures had made it in. They stood on their hind legs with their blasters raised and fixed him with their yellow stares.

Then Seb saw them: a cluster of blue barrels as tall as him and twice as wide right beside the shutter. They looked like they contained fuel.

The blaster kicked as Seb shot at the barrels, but the blue laser missed them, hitting the shutter again with another splash of orange sparks. The four creatures that had made it through into the hangar jumped to the side. Everything remained in slow motion for Seb as he tried a second shot.

This time Seb went too far the other way and blew up a small mechanic droid. The sad bot fell instantly limp from the impact.

Just before he got to the access ramp for the ship with

Sparks in it, Seb stopped, closed one eye as he looked down the sight of the blaster, and fired a third shot at the barrels. A *whoosh* sounded out when it hit and a huge fireball smothered the four beasts inside the hangar. Flames instantly drew lines around their forms as they burned, and a rush of hot air collided with him. It carried the reek of singed hair with it and hit him so hard he stumbled backwards.

The hard metal of the access ramp tapped beneath Seb's footsteps as he ran up it and entered the ship's hull. The tang of smoke rushed into the ship with him.

Sparks stood wide-eyed inside the small vessel and breathed on the edge of a panic attack. Seb grabbed her slim shoulders and shook her so hard her head snapped back and forth. The glaze lifted from her stare and she jumped to life. She moved to a wall of buttons by the ship's exit. Several quick taps and the access ramp pulled back into the ship's body with a *whir*. She then ran for the cockpit and Seb followed her.

Sparks didn't seem fazed by the wall of screens and buttons in the cockpit, but when she looked again at the fire Seb had ignited, she froze momentarily and watched it burn out.

The explosion had blown the shutter clean away from the hole, and although the fire had taken out a few of the creatures, the rest of them now charged into the hangar. Seb nudged his small friend. "Come on, Sparks, get us out of here."

A volley of blaster fire rushed at them as the beasts all reared up with their weapons. The blasts shook the ship when they connected with its metal body. With everything back to a normal speed, Seb watched Sparks shake as her fingers danced across the ship's control panel. Although he wanted to scream at her to hurry up, he bit his tongue.

The creatures continued to swarm into the hangar and sent another wave of shots their way.

The ship shook and Seb heard a fizz from where they connected with something electrical. "I don't think we can take much more of this, Sparks," he said.

Just as the third wave of fire came at them, a loud *whoom* sounded out and Seb now saw the creatures through a light blue filter. The blaster fire hit the ship's shield and diluted on impact with a wet pop.

Before the creatures could change their method of attack, Sparks grabbed the controls and lifted them a metre or so from the ground. The ship swayed as she fought for control of it.

"I thought you knew how to fly one of these things," Seb said, seeing the beasts back down on all fours and racing towards them.

"I do … in principle."

"In *principle*?"

Instead of replying, Sparks clenched her teeth. She pushed hard on the lever in front of her and the ship shot forward, throwing Seb back.

The pain of hitting the metal rear wall clattered through Seb as it jarred his skeleton and he hit the floor in a heap. Unable to stand up against the ship's hard acceleration, Seb remained where he was and watched the steel of the hangar shoot past them. Seconds later, it gave way to the void of a black star-studded sky.

Exhausted and sweating from the getaway, in pain from the fight, and still out of breath, Seb sank into his posture and managed a half-smile. "Well done, Sparks," he said, tiredness tugging on his frame. "Well done."

CHAPTER 3

"Uh … Seb?" Sparks said.

Seb opened his heavy eyelids, lethargic from the lure of sleep nearly dragging him under. After they'd taken off and he'd been flung back into one of the steel walls, he'd crawled over to a nearby padded bench and lay down on it. Everything ached from their escape, so he'd closed his eyes to let his body rest.

Before Seb could reply, Sparks repeated, "Seb?"

Seb groaned as he sat up, a deep throbbing headache pulsing inside his skull. When he saw Sparks open her mouth to call him again, he cut her off, "It's okay, I heard ya."

"Well, *answer* me then."

Seb got to his feet—his legs wobbly with exhaustion—and stumbled over to Sparks. Too tired to shout across the ship, he walked up behind her. "What do you want?"

Sparks pointed one of her long fingers down in front of her.

An entire console of lights, buttons, and levers stared back at Seb. "I don't know what any of that nonsense means. What are you pointing at?"

When Sparks tapped her long finger against a circular screen, her fingernail clicked as it connected with the glass. The screen had a blob in its centre and concentric circles surrounded it. Seb saw the pulsing dots in the bottom half of the screen and his tiredness left him. "Damn."

Without another word to Sparks, Seb ran to the back of the ship and looked out of the large rear window. The dots he'd seen on the screen manifested as a cluster of ships behind them.

"Get in the turret now," Sparks called back to him.

A hatch lay in the centre of the floor. Round and with recessed handles, Seb pulled it up to reveal a ladder in a tight tunnel. It led to the turret attached to the base of the ship.

Seb climbed down the cold metal rungs, the space so enclosed it amplified his panicked breaths as he descended.

At the bottom of the ladder, Seb dropped into the large padded seat and gripped the two blaster handles to aim the gun behind them. The turret clung to the bottom of the ship as a transparent dome. Only just large enough for him, the vessel couldn't have been native to the planet they'd just escaped from. No way would one of the ninja creatures fit into the space.

When Seb leaned left, the turret spun so quickly it made him dizzy. It did the same the other way when he leaned right to try to straighten it. With subtler movements than before, he gently encouraged the turret around so it faced the ships on their tail.

As he watched their enemies get closer, his heart on over-drive, Seb drew a deep breath to encourage everything to slow down around him.

A few seconds later nothing had changed other than the enemy ships had gotten closer. Everything moved at the same fast pace. So fast Seb saw their attackers as a blur.

Panic rose to the surface and Seb struggled to hold onto his composure. After he'd closed his eyes for a few seconds and took several more deep breaths, he opened them again, expecting the world to be slower. Nothing.

Spark's voice came through the ship's speakers, distorted from where she shouted down at him. "What are you doing, Seb? You've got to *shoot* at them."

Seb shook and his heart fought to burst free from his chest. He squeezed the triggers on the cannon's handles. The entire turret kicked with every shot and he struggled to hold it straight. Green lasers arced away from him through the darkness of space. They left traces behind them that showed how gloriously inaccurate his shots were.

"Come on, Seb, they're getting closer."

After a glance up at the speakers, Seb clenched his jaw and didn't answer her. He held on to the cannon's handles as he sent another barrage of shots out into space behind them. They missed by more than the first shots had.

A wipe of his brow did little to stem the flow of sweat and Seb flinched in his seat as the ships fired back. Their green lasers came much closer than his had, one of them running so near to him the bright glare of it left blobs of light in his vision.

Seb called on his ability again with another deep inhale and, if anything, the world around him seemed to speed up. "Come on," he shouted as he squeezed the triggers for longer than before. His accuracy hadn't improved.

The turret protruded from the ship, leaving Seb ready to be picked off like a rabbit poking its head from a hole. As that thought ran through his mind, another green bar of laser fire flared past him and he flinched away from it. "Not that flinching's going to do anything."

"Huh?" Sparks called through the ship's intercom.

Seb didn't reply.

"We won't last long like this," Sparks shouted.

Seb finally broke. "I know!" He gripped onto the handles of the gun, screamed at the top of his voice, and squeezed both triggers. The cannon shook and the turret spun left and right, spraying green fire out behind him with little accuracy.

Two bright explosions filled the sky behind them and Seb let go of the triggers. He released a relieved sigh to see two of the ships blown up, but a quick count showed him at least eight more remained on their tail.

The enemy had now gotten so close, Seb could see the yellow-eyed ninjas through the front screens of their ships. It ached his shoulders to keep the large cannon raised against the kick of each fire, but he did it and let off another wave in their direction. At least, he intended to let off another wave in their direction. The gun kicked and bucked, the laser spray utterly inaccurate as it raced away from him through the dark sky.

One ship gained on them quicker than the others. Chrome and shaped like an arrowhead, Seb watched its cannons glow as they charged.

"They're locking onto us," Sparks called to him.

Seb aimed his cannon, and just before he could squeeze the triggers, his target vanished from sight. Several more sharp turns and Sparks had shaken it from their tail.

"Seb, you need to do better. I can't outmanoeuvre all of them."

Seb didn't reply. Sparks wouldn't want to hear that he couldn't do anything without his power. She didn't even know about his power.

Two more ships came into view behind them. They sat side by side, both of their cannons glowing green with the charge of a fierce bolt.

The vibration through the cannon blurred Seb's vision as he sent more laser fire into the sky, but he missed by what felt like a mile. He slapped his palm against his head and shouted, "Damn it. Come on, Seb, get it together." But it did nothing to slow his world down. However his ability worked, it didn't work here.

"Seb! What's going on? I can't get away from them. Seb?"

The sound of Sparks' voice added to the chaos in Seb's mind and his thoughts spiraled. He let go of the cannon, covered his face with both hands, and pulled his knees up onto the seat.

Even though he had his hands over his face, Seb's world lit up green seconds before the entire ship shook. A deep *whoosh* ran through the vessel from the impact of the cannons and the already hot turret turned molten in a second.

Several loud pops and rips and Seb's sinuses filled with the reek of burning plastic. He then felt a tug on his body from the ship being torn apart, and bright light blinded him as he was dragged out into space.

CHAPTER 4

Still dazzled from the bright explosion, Seb rubbed his eyes as the lights in the simulator room came on, blinding him further. Although Sparks didn't say anything, when he looked at her, he felt her disappointment and said, "I'm sorry."

The small Thrystian batted the comment away with her long-fingered hand. Although she said the words, her eyes tightened at the edges and betrayed her sentiment. "It's fine. Don't worry about it."

Wound even tighter by her response, Seb clenched his jaw. "It's *not* fine. You did everything asked of you, if not more, and I screwed it up because I can't shoot in a dogfight."

Pity hung on Sparks' features and she said nothing in response. Not that Seb could blame her; with his current frame of mind, any conversation with him would be a waste of time and a conduit for his self-loathing rage.

Before Seb could think on it any more, Sparks walked to the simulator's exit. He sighed, his body sinking with the deep exhale. He'd have to follow her out there.

The simulator rooms took up one side of a huge underground bunker. Each one had rows of benches behind them for spectators to sit on. When Seb and Sparks had gone in, the benches were full. When they came out, Moses remained as the only one there. No doubt the rest of them had witnessed the mess their mission had been and left before things got heated.

Whenever they ran a simulation, they had to turn the lights in the bunker down low. Any glare from outside could break the illusion. Although Moses sat close to where they'd emerged from, the dark room cast a deep shadow across his face that hid most of his features. Yet Seb saw his cold eyes clearer than ever as Moses surveyed him with his usual contemptuous detachment.

As much as Seb wanted to walk past Moses and go back to his room, the large shark-like creature wouldn't stand for it. Especially when Sparks walked over and sat down next to him.

Although Moses had always been hard to read, Seb felt something in the air at that moment. The slightest spark and the big creature would blow his top.

Seb moved over to the bench and sat far enough away to be out of Moses' reach. At first, the head of the Shadow Order turned to Sparks, his tone light in his appraisal of her performance. "A-plus, Sparks, well done. You did everything you needed to do and in a timely fashion. My only criticism would be to try to hold the ship a bit steadier in the bunker. The last thing you need is an unnecessary crash while you're getting away."

Sparks nodded at Moses before lowering her purple eyes in deference. "I will do that. Thank you."

The attention of the other two then turned to Seb and he shrank even smaller than he already felt.

Moses cocked his head to the side. "What was *that*?"

Other than 'Go screw yourself, Moses,' Seb didn't have a response.

"You let us down, Seb. How many simulators will you mess up because you can't get any better in a dogfight? I'd suggest you fly the ship and let Sparks shoot, but Sparks is such a good pilot it would be a waste to have her on the guns. At least with Sparks' skills, you may stand a chance of survival. If we put *you* in the cockpit, you'd probably crash before you took off."

Heat flushed Seb's cheeks and his pulse raced. A torrent of fury built up inside him, but he held his tongue.

Moses must have wanted a response because he tutted when he didn't get one and shooed Seb away with his hand. "Go and watch Gurt and the Silent Assassin to see how it's done. Hopefully, you'll learn something from them."

Seb walked over to the observation area for the simulator next to them. Gurt—a Mandulu who could shoot the pimple off a baby's bottom—had the Silent Assassin as his team-mate. They aced every simulator they tried and Gurt made sure Seb knew about it.

As Gurt and SA's virtual mission played out in front of them, Seb watched his and Sparks' escape on the monitor above the simulation room they'd been in. It played as a replay until someone switched it off. That could take days because Moses believed in everyone learning from one another. And to be fair, Seb and Sparks aced their escape for the most part. Everything went well until they had to engage in a dogfight—the story of so many of their simulations.

A heavy nudge nearly knocked Seb from the bench. When he looked at Moses next to him, the shark-like creature spoke through a face full of sharp and clenched teeth. "Focus on *this* simulator. You might learn something."

The clock on the screen showed Gurt and the Silent Assassin arriving at the hangar at about the same time as Seb and Sparks had. The combined fighting force of the two saw them dispatch their pursuers with ease, but they didn't have Sparks' skills for hot-wiring the motor on the shutter. Instead, Gurt fired what seemed to be over a hundred shots at the hangar's doorframe. Made from rock, the frame crumbled and the shutter fell forward and crashed on the ground.

SA got the ship started while Gurt stood in the hangar's doorway and used his blasters to see off the next wave of attackers.

The beasts barely made it through the gap in the rocks before Gurt dispatched them, every one of his shots scoring a direct hit from over fifty metres away.

The second Gurt entered the ship, he went straight to the gunner's turret and SA flew them out of the hangar. They picked a different ship than Seb and Sparks had—a larger one. The pilot had to take responsibility for making sure the vessel would be appropriate for their needs. SA had to be certain Gurt could fit in the turret.

Seb squinted when he looked at the faraway dots. "Are they—?"

Gurt confirmed it for Seb when he let seven blasts free and seven explosions responded in the distance.

The last of the exploded ships died out and the lights in Gurt and SA's simulator suddenly came on. The abrupt change dazzled Seb for the second time that day.

The simulator room turned white as the projection vanished. Gurt and SA stood in the middle of the sparse space. After a high five, they exited the simulator.

A grin as wide as his fat jaw, Gurt looked at his spectators and said, "And that's how you do it."

When he caught Moses' eye, he smiled. Moses acknowledged his pride with a gentle nod.

Seb didn't need to feel any worse, but that never stopped Gurt, who walked over and sat down next to him on the bench. "So how did you do?"

At that moment, the replay of Seb's simulation showed him and Sparks in the ship. When the screen filled with the white light of their ship's explosion, Gurt pulled a sharp breath in and winced away from the image. He laughed. "Wow, not so good, then."

Fire spread beneath Seb's cheeks and he looked at SA. He didn't see the same derisive joy on her face. He didn't see much on her face, to be fair.

In the few weeks Seb had been at the Shadow Order's training camp, SA hadn't said a word. A tall and sleek female with yellow skin, she stood about the same height as him, just over six feet tall. She had the grace of a cat and the bite of a cobra. She could fly as well as Sparks, if not better, and her knives seemed like an extension of her limbs when she engaged in hand-to-hand combat. Not even Seb would fight her if she had her blades on her, which she always did.

When SA had trained to fight as a child, she'd taken a vow of silence. She'd only speak when she had something worth saying. Something worthy of the time and effort her masters had put into her training. Otherwise, she'd shut up and learn.

Hard to read, SA's brilliant blue eyes drank Seb in, and for the first time since he'd messed up his simulation, he felt calm.

A firm shove from Gurt forced Seb from his moment of serenity and the brute said, "Don't ignore me."

Seb's world slipped into slow motion and he jumped to his feet.

When Gurt stood up with him, Seb stepped forward. Before it could go any further, Sparks jumped up and stood between the two. They both ignored her as they continued to push against one another.

A blinding pain roared to life in Seb's thigh and pulled his groin muscles tight in a spasm. The shock of it launched him backwards and he landed on the hard floor on his back. The spot where Sparks had electrocuted him on his right thigh burned and his quads twitched. Gurt—who had fallen away in the opposite direction—looked equally as shocked by Sparks' intervention. The tiny Thrystian simply shrugged while she looked from one of them to the other. "You two don't need to be fighting."

"I beg to differ," Seb replied, wincing as he forced his words out past the pain Sparks had inflicted on him.

Before Gurt could respond, Moses stepped between them and addressed Seb. "Gurt has every right to call you out on your performance, you know."

Instead of replying, Seb got back to his feet and looked across the large bunker to see a crowd of about fifty recruits had gathered to watch.

Moses then moved so close Seb could smell the antiseptic reek of his cologne. His deep voice rattled against Seb's chest. "Your dogfights are pathetic. You're going to get yourself and your team killed if you don't get any better. We've been practicing and practicing, and if anything, you've gotten worse."

Fury bubbled beneath Seb's skin and he felt every pair of eyes in the place on him. He kept his attention on the dark blue floor and said nothing.

Moses stepped even closer and shoved Seb in the chest; it sent Seb stumbling backwards, his weakened right leg giving way beneath him as he fell on his arse again.

The contact with the hard floor shook through Seb and he bit his tongue on impact. The metallic taste of his own blood filled his mouth, and before he could think, his world had slowed down, he'd jumped to his feet, and he'd rushed back towards Moses.

About a metre away from the large creature, Seb stopped when Moses pulled out a blaster and pointed it straight at his face. What had seemed like a lot of teeth doubled when Moses bared them. He seemed to be struggling to keep his voice even, his chest rising and falling with his quick breaths as he said, "You need to keep your mood in check, boy."

In the face of Moses' obsidian glare, Seb's world returned to a normal speed. A vacuum for emotion, Moses' eyes sucked him into a black hole. If Moses wanted it, Seb would disappear forever. He needed to remember that.

"Now, I like you, Seb," Moses said, "but I won't have anyone getting in my face like that. You got me?"

Heavy breaths helped calm Seb down. When he glanced across at Gurt, the Mandulu flashed him a facetious smile.

Because Seb hadn't replied, Moses stepped closer to him and spoke slowly. "Have. You. Got. Me?"

Another deep breath and Seb fought to keep the petulance from his tone when he said, "Yep."

After Moses lowered his gun, Seb walked past him and left the bunker.

CHAPTER 5

J ust as the elevator doors were closing, Sparks jumped sideways through them and joined Seb inside. Made from chrome, the elevator had just two buttons: one for up top and one for the complex below. Seb had already pressed the button to take him up top.

The doors closed completely and Seb's stomach lurched a little as the elevator rose. For the first few seconds, they stood in silence before Seb said, "I don't know how much more of this I can take."

"Do you think you have a choice?"

Already tense, Seb wound even tighter. "*What?*"

Although only small, Sparks stood fierce in her assertions and stared back at him. "If you can put your ego to one side for a minute, you *might* actually be able to think straight."

Seb breathed through his nose and ground his teeth.

"Well, think about it. Where did we escape from to get here?"

Seb didn't respond.

"And where will they send us if we don't want to be here?"

"I wonder if a cell would be better than the crap we have to put up with in this place."

"Just think about the money, Seb. You ain't getting performance-based pay. We just have to do a year or two in the Shadow Order, and then we can go wherever we like."

"We?"

"*You* can go wherever you like. Don't worry; I've already spent enough time with you. I've got plans of my own."

Silence filled the small elevator again and Seb looked everywhere but at Sparks. Not that the chrome walls had much to look at. "Why did you come in here with me? I wanted to be alone."

"Because I wanted to make sure you're okay."

"And if I'm not? What can *you* do about it?"

An impish glee lit up Sparks' purple eyes. "I can help you continue the argument. Because that's how we fix things, isn't it? We get angry with anyone who gets in the way and shout until the matter's resolved. That's how all great debates are settled, right?"

Seb sighed.

When the elevator doors opened, the salty and wet wind rushed in and blew Seb's hair back. He'd been on Aloo before and he'd hated the weather, but now he lived beneath the sea in a space filled with recycled air and artificial light, coming up to Aloo's surface often helped level him out. Blasted by the elements, he spread his arms wide and inhaled the cold force of nature as it battered him and left the taste of salt in his mouth.

On the opposite pole to the spaceport, the Shadow Order's base remained one of Aloo's greatest secrets. Anyone who ever visited believed the spaceport to be its only patch of land. Moses went to great lengths to make sure it stayed that way.

The large metal surface served as the landing pad for their base and sat like a huge coin in the sea. The water surrounding it rose and fell. It splashed against the sides as the waves broke on it. Sometimes the storms got so rough, the platform ended up completely submerged. When that happened, the lifts would lock down and nobody could leave the base.

Every time Seb came up to the surface, the motion of the waves made him dizzy as he rocked with them in the constantly shifting environment.

Now Seb had had a few minutes to calm down, he turned to Sparks, who looked out over the sea. "I'm sorry," he said. "I just can't control my temper sometimes."

Sparks pulled her razor-sharp bob from her face with one of her long fingers and remained deadpan. "I hadn't noticed."

Seb couldn't help but smile.

"Look, I understand why you feel how you do. It's rubbish that we're not getting the simulations nailed—"

"*I'm* not getting them nailed, Sparks," Seb interrupted.

"We're a team. I take the hit with you. I may not get the dressing down that you do, but I feel the loss heavily too."

The salt-sting in Seb's eyes burned stronger when the clouds parted and the sun's glare dazzled him. It bounced off the vast expanse of water as if it were a huge mirror.

"We just need to practice more," Sparks said. "We'll get there."

"We'd best do. I think Moses will send us on a mission soon."

"Look," Sparks said, "I know you probably don't feel like going back down below for a while, but it won't get any easier. In fact, it'll only get harder the longer you stay away from everyone else. At least if we go back now, we can get some food in the canteen."

Sparks tugged on Seb's arm as she moved back toward the elevator in the centre of the platform.

Reluctant at first, Seb gave in and followed her.

CHAPTER 6

The elevator reacted to Seb and Sparks' close proximity to it by rising from the flat platform with a gentle *whir* and opening its doors. Seb watched Sparks enter, but he remained still. Rocked on the balls of his feet by the elements, his eyes still stinging, and the taste of salt drying his mouth, he watched the tiny Sparks stare back at him with her hands on her hips. He drew a deep sigh. Although he wanted to remain up top a little longer, it wouldn't be worth the hassle she'd undoubtedly give him. He followed her into the small elevator.

After the doors closed, Seb looked around the tight chrome space, the smell of disinfectant in the air. "Do you think the elevator is this size for a reason? Or do you think they built it and then realised they'd excluded all of the larger species from joining the Shadow Order simply by restricting their access to the base?"

Sparks clicked her tongue and looked around the inside of the elevator too. "Well, I suppose you have to make a decision on size at some point. And even if some of the bigger species could get down into the base, they wouldn't be able to pilot any of the ships because they wouldn't fit in them. If you want an organisation built on espionage, I don't suppose a large lumbering Walldat would be much use anyway."

It made sense.

Sparks ruffled her nose. "They should consider themselves lucky they don't have to cope with this smell too."

"I asked Moses why the lift always stank," Seb said.

"And?"

"The elevator cleans itself when it can. Because it has to open up to the elements of Aloo whenever it goes up top, it self-cleans when it closes. It washes away all the salt so it doesn't corrode over time."

The description seemed to bore Sparks, who looked like she'd switched off to Seb's explanation. After he'd pulled his sodden hair from his eyes, he looked at his quiet friend. "Are you okay?"

"Huh?" Sparks asked, a deep frown hooding her purple eyes.

While clicking his fingers at her as if to get her attention, he said, "Aloo calling Sparks, come in, Sparks."

After a shake of her head, a touch of clarity returned to Sparks' eyes. "You weren't the only one of our team who found the simulator hard."

"No, but I was the one who messed it up."

"I nearly did too."

"Stop trying to make me feel better, Sparks."

"I'm not, trust me. Moses noticed it, and I think you would have were you not so involved in the escape."

Although Seb cast his mind back and he remembered Moses saying something to Sparks, he couldn't recall what exactly. So ashamed of his performance, he'd found himself lost in his own hole of negativity.

"The ship," Sparks said. "I nearly crashed the ship."

"But that was you getting the hang of the controls."

"I had the hang of the controls. I can fly most things with my eyes closed. It wasn't that, it was the fire."

The lift continued to plunge down into the Shadow Order's base. It ran deep to get to the bottom of the ocean. Seb's heart fluttered and his chest tightened as if he could feel the vast pressure of water that pushed against the base's outer frame. One weak spot anywhere and ... He shoved the thought to the back of his mind and returned to the memory of the simulator, drawing a blank. "What fire?"

"Do you remember shooting the barrels of rocket fuel?"

"Ah! Of course, *that* fire."

"I hate fire." Sparks' eyes—magnified by her glasses— spread wide. "Why do you think I ran when the balrog chased us?"

"Uh ... because a balrog was chasing us."

"Fair point. But it's more than that. When I was on Thryst, I was caught in a house fire. One of the few times I'd made a friend on that cursed planet, the two of us ended up trapped in the attic of a shop. Amelia was younger than me by a few years and she looked up to me. I befriended her because I found her on the streets trying to survive like I had. She needed some guidance. An orphan at a young age, she recognised she'd be better trying her luck on the streets than trusting the authorities."

As Seb took in the distant look in Sparks' eyes, his mouth hung open and his breathing slowed down to an almost halt. "So what happened?"

"One of the beams in the attic dropped between us. It was burning white hot within seconds. I couldn't do anything about it. Even if it weren't on fire, I didn't have the strength to lift it, and there wasn't the space to get past it. We stared at one another for a few seconds before she threw her computer to me." At that moment, glassy-eyed with grief and slightly lost in her tale, Sparks held her computer up. "Amelia taught me everything I know about hacking and programming. Not only did she give me permission to leave her that day, but she also gave me the ability to thrive in this universe. The only window out of the attic was on my side, so I climbed out of it. The second I got out onto the roof, it sounded like the flames got her. She screamed like nothing I've ever heard before. It was a primal noise as if demons had possessed her. By the time I'd made it down to the street, her screaming had stopped. Thick dark smoke billowed out of the window I'd escaped from, and I swear I could smell her burned flesh."

It felt strange to comfort his small friend because they didn't have that kind of relationship, but Seb put a hand on Sparks' slim shoulder anyway. "I'm so sorry you had to go through that."

"I waited a few blocks away and listened to the fire ships arrive to put the fire out. Amelia's last words to me were 'Go, and don't let them catch you'. With no chance of saving her, she wanted to make sure I got far away so I didn't get taken in by the authorities."

Seb exhaled hard, deflating as he considered Sparks' loss.

"Anyway," Sparks said, "fire freaks me out."

"I think it would freak me out too if I had witnessed that."

"And Moses saw that in the simulation," Sparks said. "He may not have said it, but he saw it. It was lucky I managed to hold it together."

"I don't think it's luck." Seb pulled her into him in a one-armed hug. "I think you're a tough cookie. You have one of the most level heads I've ever come across, you're super smart, and you're brave."

Stepping out of her memories, Sparks' purple eyes cleared and she stared up at Seb. "Thank you."

Seb dipped a nod at her.

"It's happening again, you know? Despite me promising myself it wouldn't."

Although Seb waited for Sparks to elaborate, she didn't. "What's happening again?"

"You're making me like you. Since Amelia died, I promised myself I would never befriend anyone else. Friendships are too painful and I don't want to be vulnerable like that again. But you've broken through."

After she punched him on the arm, hard enough for it to sting, the tiny Sparks scowled at Seb. "You'd best not bloody die on me now."

"I'll try not to."

When the lift stopped, Sparks removed her glasses, wiped her eyes, and drew a deep breath.

The doors opened and Seb stared out into the hallway in front of them. From where he stood, he could see the hangar with the simulators and his pulse quickened.

"Just keep your head, okay?" Sparks said. "It doesn't matter what Gurt says, just try to remember he wants to wind you up."

A glance down at Sparks, and Seb pulled his shoulders back. "Thanks for coming up after me. I needed it."

Sparks smiled and said, "I know," before she stepped out of the elevator.

CHAPTER 7

Unlike the canteen on *The Bandolin*, the Shadow Order's canteen got cleaned regularly, had a fraction of the people in it, and served amazing food. Seb stood in line with Sparks, ignored the people around him, and focused on the menu. Pasta bake, roast dinner, curried snarch … thankfully they didn't have sea slug on the list. Just the thought of it threatened to send a heave through his stomach.

At the front of the queue, Seb's mouth watered at the sight of the slabs of raw zubber steak. Every other option ceased to exist. He pointed at one and smiled at the chef—a dirty-looking female with a huge stubbled chin—giddy in anticipation of his lunch. "Can I have one of them, please?"

"Bloody, burned, or cremated?" she asked. Her girth stretched wider than her height, and she had three eyes in her fat face. Each one assessed Seb with impatience.

"Bloody."

The chef nodded, picked the meat up in a pair of tongs, and dropped it on the griddle behind her. Flames rose up and the fat hissed. The air filled with the rich smell of cooking meat.

Sparks opted for fish with grains, which the chef also threw on the griddle.

Like *The Bandolin*, the Shadow Order's canteen had been arranged with benches that stretched across the room. The most efficient way to utilise the space, the long rows ran through it in neat lines.

One half of the canteen got used by the R and D guys, while the fighters took the other half. The fighters' section rotated often. Sometimes it would be fairly busy, while at others, there didn't seem to be many people there at all. Probably out on missions … or dead.

As Seb took in the place, he did his best to ignore Gurt's watchful eye, but, inevitably, he met the stare of the Mandulu.

"Just ignore him," Sparks said, speaking from the side of her mouth.

"He's such a smug git though."

"And you think you can change that?"

Seb didn't reply. Instead, he looked at SA. Although she sat with Gurt, the serene assassin seemed more occupied with her lunch than Gurt's bullshit. As she chewed her food—her delicate mouth closed and barely moving—Seb sighed. The woman even ate gracefully.

She looked up and Seb nearly looked away, but instead he stared back at her and fought to banish the scowl Gurt had put on his face. Her bioluminescent blue eyes drank him in and her expression changed ever so subtly, almost as if to smile, or at least to think about it.

Seb nearly smiled back until Sparks shoved him and broke him from his trance. When he looked at his friend, she pointed at the angry chef, who held a plate toward him. Heat flushed his cheeks as he took it and said, "Sorry. Thank you."

The chef had taken the liberty of plating his steak with

fried slices of a root vegetable called fairy knuckle squash. They served them often in the canteen. Unlike more traditional root vegetable chips, they seemed to get crispier than most on the outside and as fluffy as a cloud in the middle.

While Seb waited for Sparks to take her lunch, he picked up a tray for each of them, handed one to Sparks, and they both walked over to the benches to sit down to eat.

Of course, they had to pass Gurt on their way to their seat. A glow ran through the Mandulu's red eyes and a wide grin spread across his bulbous jaw. His overbite pushed his broken horns up over his leathery top lip. "Careful, SA," Gurt said to the yellow-skinned assassin, "if he thinks you've got a gun, he might panic and drop his lunch."

Sat with a board-straight back, SA didn't reply. But then, she never replied. Not that it stopped Gurt's loud guffawing; the idiot found his own jokes so funny he didn't need anyone else's approval. Despite the urge to smash his tray over Gurt's fat head, Seb resisted as he continued past him and the beautiful assassin.

Seb lifted a chip from his plate and chewed on it. The perfect mix of a little bit of salt, a crusty outer edge, and a fluffy centre made his mouth water. "How does the chef do it every time?" he asked Sparks.

Before Sparks could reply, a big, thick tree trunk of a leg shot out in front of Seb and he tripped over it. Everything flipped into slow motion, and although he didn't fall, he watched his tray fly through the air, the plate lift from the tray, and all of his food lift from the plate. As the steak took on its own trajectory, his heart sank.

Before his dinner had crashed to the floor, Seb turned to Gurt and threw his arms wide.

The large Mandulu—still in slow motion—got to his feet

as the tray smashed down. Although Gurt's chin stood prominent in Seb's vision, he got distracted by a weak spot on the Mandulu's right knee. It had to be a hidden injury. It looked like it wouldn't take much to ruin it for good.

Seb returned his attention to the Gurt's chin. Best to knock the fool out than to paralyse him permanently, regardless of how much he hated him.

With more time to think than anyone else, Seb looked at the people in the canteen. Most of the R and D department seemed to be taking their break at that point, and—like the other staff and the few Shadow Order recruits there—they all looked at Seb and Gurt.

Despite taking deep breaths, Seb couldn't calm his pulse. It boomed as a wet swell through his temples. Fists curled into balls and his jaw locked tight, he readied himself to swing for his nemesis.

Just before he attacked Gurt, Seb caught the blue flash of Sparks' taser. When he looked down at his small friend, he saw her standing with the plastic device in her hand and one eyebrow raised. She'd use it on him if she had to. Anything to make sure he didn't fight Gurt.

The world instantly returned to a normal speed and Seb stepped away. Another look at those in the canteen and one final glance at SA, and he shook his head. "You're a waste of space."

"A waste of space would be someone working for an intergalactic team that couldn't shoot straight in a dogfight. Oh … wait …"

The sides of Seb's vision blurred again and his heart raced. He forced away the slowing down of his world and walked past both his spilled dinner and the arrogant Mandulu. It took all he had to refrain from kicking his weak knee and putting the dumb creature out of the Shadow Order for good.

Although Seb didn't look around, he recognised the only sound in the silence as the gentle tap of Sparks' footsteps as she followed him out of the canteen.

CHAPTER 8

Seb stepped into his cubed room and shivered. He couldn't ever find comfort in the small space. Tracks ran along the plain chrome walls to allow the room to form into several different arrangements. A panel had been screwed into the wall opposite the door. Covered in buttons and lights, it glowed different colours in response to different requests.

Because of the sparseness of the small room, the sound of Seb's boots echoed in the hard and empty space as he strode over to the buttons. A large green one read 'Living Room' on its plastic front, so he pressed it. A circle had been marked on the floor, which Seb currently stood in. Sparks ran over to join him. As soon as she stepped into it, the entire panel turned red to indicate they shouldn't move. Whirs and clicks sounded out and the room came to life. As long as they remained within the circle, it would transform without any problems.

First, a gap opened up in the wall opposite them and a three-seater sofa slid out. Then, a panel glided across another wall to reveal a large-screen television. Next, two small tables rose from the floor on either side of the sofa. Each had a lamp turned down low. A rug fell from the ceiling, blew out a gust of wind as it dropped, and landed perfectly in the centre of the room with a loud *plop*. Finally, the lighting dipped to suit the ambiance of the space.

Once the setup had been completed, the red glow to the panel of buttons turned green, allowing Seb and Sparks to exit the circle. They both walked straight to the soft sofa and fell onto it.

As Seb sank into the comfy cushions, he stared straight ahead. A music video played out on the television. The singer —a female with what looked like large flaccid horns hanging down either side of her head all the way to her shoulders— pranced about like a pony as she sang. "What planet is *she* from?" he asked.

Sparks continued to watch the screen and offered him a lethargic shrug. She then turned to look at him. "You did well to walk away from the canteen."

Just the mention of the canteen increased Seb's pulse. "*What?* I would have done well to knock Gurt out. But you didn't give me that choice, did you?"

"If you'd have done that, you'd be kicked out of this program. They'd send you back to *The Black Hole*. Gurt wants you to lose your temper. If you didn't threaten him so much, then maybe he wouldn't give a damn. Whatever it is you have, it rattles him."

With his attention still on the screen, Seb said, "I've always fought since I was a little kid."

Although Seb could feel Sparks continue to look at him, she didn't respond.

"Bernard Hendricks was two years older than me and he went for me every single day. At lunchtime, he'd go out of his way to barge into me and intimidate me." The thought of his days at school and the humiliation he felt because of how

Bernard treated him raised Seb's body temperature. "I finally snapped. I lost it and beat the crap out of him. It felt amazing. I realised I was good at fighting from that day. I'd found my talent."

"Beating people up?"

"More than that. I was *good* at it. Hell, I *am* good at it."

"I can't argue with that," Sparks said.

The words almost stuck in Seb's throat, but he forced them out. If he could pick someone to tell all of this to for the first time, Sparks seemed like the best person. "It's more than just being able to fight."

Sparks laughed and turned back to the bright television opposite them. "What, like a superpower or something?"

Seb looked at her, and when she looked back, the smile fell from her face.

"I think the ability comes from my mum," Seb said. "She wasn't human, although she looked it. She wouldn't tell me which planet she came from."

Sparks' mouth hung open as she looked at Seb, but she didn't reply.

"My brother has my abilities too, or at least, I think he does. I don't think my dad had them. I've never spoken about this to anyone before."

"You're not really speaking to me about it either," Sparks said. "I can see you want to tell me something, but you're being very cryptic."

A deep breath and Seb flushed hot. He looked at Sparks and opened his mouth, but the words didn't come. Her wide-eyed anticipation of what he had to say threw him off, so he stared at his lap. "When I fight, time slows down."

Silence.

"Sounds crazy, right? But it does."

Silence.

"Whenever I'm in that fighting state, my opponents move like they're stuck in treacle. Also, I can see the weak spots on them and know exactly where to hit them."

Sparks seemed to mull over what he'd said before she replied. "That makes sense." She looked him up and down. "No offence, but I did wonder how you won fights you shouldn't have. I can tell you, it's pretty impressive to watch. Dizzying even."

It would probably sound arrogant to admit that he'd like to see it from her perspective, but having only ever seen his fights through his own eyes, he constantly wondered how it looked from the outside.

A shift again on the sofa and Sparks leaned toward Seb. "Why haven't you told anyone before?"

"I dunno; it's just never come up, I suppose. Also, I don't want to get banned from the fighting pits. Until just recently, that was how I made my money. I may need to go back to them at some point. And"—Seb turned his hands over one another—"I've never had anyone I can trust enough before."

From the briefest glance at Sparks, Seb saw her eyes fill with tears. He continued, "I don't know how long I can go on letting Gurt embarrass me like he has been. Every time he goads me, the world slows down and all I want to do is lay him out. I'm not sure I can resist the urge forever."

Despite the size of the sofa and the gap separating them, when Sparks reached across, her long fingers easily touched Seb's arm. "You're doing so well. I've wanted to attack Gurt and he barely knows I exist. I don't know how you're keeping your head, but it takes a stronger person to do that than it does to lose their temper. Think about all of the times you've lost your rag in the past, that's the easy part. But showing restraint …"

A slideshow of memories flashed through Seb's mind. In

every one of them, he stood victorious over some creature. Some of the fights started for ridiculous reasons like something as trivial as a spilled drink. The memories left a dull lump as a rock in his guts. "Despite the rush of the fight, I often feel empty afterwards. Unless I'm fighting to save someone's life or I'm in the pits. Then I feel like it's what I'm supposed to do."

Although Sparks opened her mouth to respond, Seb said, "But the problem I'm having when we simulate dogfights is that my power doesn't work. That's why we keep on failing. Everything seems to move so fast, I just can't keep track of it. I don't know what I'll do when we get in that situation for real."

Sparks held her bottom lip in a pinch as if she'd be able to think up an answer for him. "I don't know either, but we'll work something out. There's nothing we can't overcome as a team."

The statement sounded about as empty as the feeling that occupied Seb's stomach, and he shrugged. What could Sparks do to help him shoot better? Their current failings rested squarely on his shoulders. "I'm sorry to be a bore, Sparks, but it's been a long day. I just want to go to bed now. I know it's a pain for you because you'll have to go to bed too."

"Are you okay if I stay on the sofa to watch television?" Sparks asked.

Seb nodded.

Sparks grabbed her mini-computer and tapped it so it came to life. Her fingers skittered over the touch screen and the panel on the wall cycled through a series of colours in response. A few seconds later the sofa shifted forward with Seb and Sparks on it. The bunkbeds they slept in rose from the floor behind them.

Despite his dark mood, Seb laughed. "The things you can do with that thing."

Sparks shrugged. "It's a handy tool for sure."

Without another word, Seb stood up on the sofa and used it as a step to get into bed. The second he lay down on the top bunk, he let his exhausted body sink into the soft mattress and dread ran through him. Maybe he shouldn't have told Sparks about his ability. Maybe she'd use it against him at some point. Maybe she'd lied to him about being friends in the elevator and she'd just pulled on his heart strings to understand his secrets. It didn't really matter; he'd told her now and he couldn't take that back. He'd have to trust her.

Seb rolled over onto his side, put his back to the television, and faced the shiny steel wall. Each blink stayed closed longer than the last, and the sound of bad pop music from across the galaxy took him into a dream state.

CHAPTER 9

S eb walked with Sparks toward the hangar that housed the simulators. The worry that he'd shared his secret with someone had slightly duller claws after a good night's sleep. If he could trust anyone in this life, she walked next to him at that moment. Although they'd not started off on the best footing, experience had soldered their connection to one another. Not only a recruitment tool, the prison break had forged a twosome as tight as any brothers or sisters in arms.

Although still early, when they walked into the hangar, a group of the other recruits had already gathered there. About twenty of them in total, the slight hum of chatter that had bubbled between them died down, leaving just the sound of Seb's and Sparks' feet over the hard floor.

"This seems a bit weird," Seb said, shielding his mouth, but speaking loud enough to make sure he'd been heard.

Sparks looked at him but didn't respond.

Despite his cocky show of disregard, Seb's breaths came quicker. He'd never felt comfortable with the attention of so many people on him unless he was about to fight. "I reckon they're all looking at us because I did so gloriously badly yesterday. What do you think?"

Several raised eyebrows—or facial expressions close to that for the eyebrow-less contingent in the group—looked their way. Again, Sparks didn't reply.

"Maybe we're in the simulators again today. Having only just been put on them, I'm sure we're going to be given another chance for me to mess it up." Seb laughed, the echo in the room making him face just how forced his humour sounded.

When the gathered creatures still didn't react, Seb forced another chuckle. "Wow. Tough crowd."

Seb and Sparks stopped just a few metres before they got to the group. The Shadow Order recruits had to meet every morning in the hangar to be given their daily training routine. So while today looked just like any other day, the atmosphere in the place felt vastly different. Or maybe it didn't. It could simply be that Seb viewed himself through the perceived judgment of his peers. Surely none of them cared about the incredibly public display of his ineptitude as much as he did.

For the first time since he'd met the ugly beast, Seb felt grateful for Gurt's arrival and his complete lack of awareness. His loud voice scythed through the tense atmosphere with the subtlety of a pulse cannon skinning a peach. "Oi oi. Look what we have here; the human that couldn't shoot straight, no matter how hard he tried."

Seb's gratitude faded almost instantly when half of the deadpan group sniggered.

Clearly spurred on by the reaction, Gurt smiled, his horns lifting with his fat face. "And he's got his ratty sidekick with him, the goggle-eyed geek."

A few more creatures laughed and one of them—a blue-skinned tsunab from the watery planet Nami—turned their back on Seb and Sparks to try to hide his mirth.

Gurt could attack Seb as much as he liked; he deserved it, in fact. But when he looked at the now crimson-faced Sparks, he balled his hands into fists. "Leave Sparks out of it."

Gurt stopped, and for the first time Seb noticed SA behind him. The embodiment of both grace and stealth, she moved away from her teammate, soundless in her delicate steps. Gurt didn't seem to have any awareness of SA's actions and he laughed. "Hit a nerve, have I?"

The crowd of creatures stepped back. Although Seb didn't reply, he stared straight into the Mandulu's red eyes. Adrenaline ran through his blood like rocket fuel, so when Gurt blew him a kiss with his leathery lips, he marched toward him. Sparks grabbed his arm on the way past, but he shook her off and continued straight for the large beast.

Everything slowed down as Seb got closer to Gurt. The weak spot on both Gurt's large chin and right knee remained crystal clear while the periphery of Seb's vision blurred into a watercoloured mix. Nothing other than him and Gurt mattered at that moment.

Despite balling his fists, when Seb stepped close to the large creature, he resisted the urge to swing for him.

Like every Mandulu, Gurt stank. A heady mix of body odour and flatulence, the creature's skin glistened from the waxy secretion he sweated out. Anywhere else but there and Seb would have laid him out by that point.

Although Gurt spoke, Seb couldn't make any sense of his slowed-down words. He had most of his attention on the brute's weak chin.

The slow motion made the grip on Seb's left shoulder a million times worse. What would have been a sharp sting dragged out into a burning, elongated spasm. The muscles in his neck pulled tight and he snapped his left ear down to his left shoulder to try to counter the pain as someone pulled him backwards.

When Seb spun around, ready to swing, he saw who had him, lost his fight, and his world returned to a normal speed.

Were Seb to fight Moses, he'd probably knock him out, but the battle didn't matter because he'd never win the war against him.

The shark-like beast stared down at Seb, detached as he looked at him with his cold onyx glare. One of Moses' fingers sat as wide as three of Seb's, and he pointed it straight at him and then Gurt. "You two, in the simulator *now*. You've been at each other's throats ever since you got here. I don't know why you have such a problem with one another, but you need to settle it today."

The grin on Gurt's face spread wider than before as he looked at Seb. "I've been waiting for this."

Seb clenched his jaw so tightly a dull ache ran up either side of his face. "You're not the only one, you dumb primate."

Gurt's smile fell and he stepped forward, but Moses shoved him back with a hard push against his chest. Gurt looked like he'd fight back until Moses bared his teeth. White and razor sharp, they occupied half of his wide head.

Gurt dipped his gaze in submission as he and Seb followed Moses to the simulator.

CHAPTER 10

Before the lights outside the simulator turned off, Seb looked around at the crowd. In the short time it had taken him and Gurt to enter the small room, it seemed like the entire complex had turned up to watch. But only two people mattered to him at that moment: Sparks, who'd managed to snake her way into the front row—not that it surprised him; the girl could get in and out of anywhere—and SA, who stood as a picture of serenity, statuesque amongst the excitement of the rest of the spectators. Her bright blue eyes lit up in the dark as she watched, and he savoured the moment.

Within seconds, the illusion of the simulator would drag Seb under and he'd have zero recollection of reality beyond the fabricated experience. Whatever world Moses had planned for them, it would seem real until he got pulled back out of it. Hopefully he'd return with his pride intact for once.

An image of Moses materialised in front of Seb and Gurt and the spectators behind disappeared from view as the simulator switched on. Suddenly Seb found himself standing in what seemed to be a rainforest. Vibrant and green, humidity hung in the hot air and instantly pressed against his skin like sweat. He inhaled the smell of tropical flowers and listened to the cacophony of bird songs all around him. Moses raised a small screen and turned it to show the two of them. Seb couldn't help but smile when he saw the image on it. It stood tall, poking from the forest as a vast stone structure.

"You can't see it from here," Moses said, "but at the end of this jungle is a fighting pit. That's your destination. The first one there will have longer to rest than the other. The second you both enter the ring, you fight."

A cocky grin, and the Mandulu said, "Yeah, but what's stopping me taking a casual stroll over there to conserve my energy?" He then looked at Seb, arched an eyebrow, and snorted a laugh. "Not that I need to worry about conserving my energy so I can fight this rat." The fake bravado didn't convince Seb. Gurt knew he could brawl, just like he knew Gurt could shoot.

Seb followed Moses' line of sight and turned around to look behind him. Two huge beasts stood in cages. Each metal prison stretched at least three stories high and just as wide. Despite the size of their cells, the creatures didn't look like they had much space to move.

The beasts appeared to be identical. Both were the size of small ships and they seemed to want nothing more than to get at Seb and Gurt. Huge powerful forearms like gorillas, they looked like they could crush a skull like Seb would an egg.

In reaction to Seb and Gurt looking at them, both of the creatures screamed. The shrill call cut through Seb and forced his shoulders up against his neck in an involuntary spasm. The birds fell silent around them. When the beasts stretched their mouths wide, they showed they could swallow Seb or Gurt whole.

Regardless of his fighting ability, Seb would have a hard time overcoming one of the brutes. If he wanted to get to the pit, he'd have to stay ahead of the two monsters. Nothing short of outrunning them would suffice. A glance at Gurt, and he saw he'd turned pale. "Not so smug now, eh?" He looked down at Gurt's weak knee.

A sneer lifted one side of Gurt's fat mouth. "Just you wait, *human*. You won't know what's hit you when we get to the pit."

Of everything that had occurred since they'd joined the Shadow Order, Seb felt pretty certain of what would happen in a fighting pit. He said nothing to the Mandulu. Let him find out when they got there. *If* they got there.

"Ready?" Moses called out.

Although Seb didn't acknowledge him, he crouched down, the desire to run coiled in his tight leg muscles.

"Go!"

The rattle of the cage doors sounded out behind them as Seb exploded to life.

A sheet of vines hung down in front of Seb and obscured his view of what lay beyond them. He charged straight through them and found a wall on the other side.

Seb looked left and right as he pressed against the cold rock. He'd run into a dead end already.

The screams of the two beasts closed down on them. It ran ice through Seb and he nearly froze until he saw Gurt climb one of the vines. It sparked him to life and he copied Gurt's actions.

The rough vines cut Seb's hands, and a mixture of sweat and moisture in the air both stung the open cuts on his palms and made it harder to grip on. But he kept going, and once he'd reached about halfway, he overtook Gurt. With the sound of the monster's steps closing in on them, he looked down. About twenty metres between him and the hard ground; if he slipped now …

Still a little way away, Seb saw the huge hairy forms of the two monsters moving through the humid forest. The brush gave way to their charge, and when one of them hit a tree, a loud tear of ripping wood creaked through the space and the tree fell with an almighty crash.

As he ascended the vine, Seb felt the vibrations of the monsters' stomping feet. The one on his tail did exactly as he'd done; it ran beneath him to the dead end of the wall.

Seb looked down on the top of its vast and hairy head. Although it hadn't looked up, the beast's movement had disturbed the vine enough for Seb to have to hold on tighter as it swung. Trickier with the aggravated movement, he continued his climb regardless.

About three-quarters of the way up the vine, Seb couldn't tell if his palms were wet because of blood or sweat. The humid rainforest had made his entire body slick with perspiration and his eyes stung as the salty secretion ran into them. Yet every pull up the rope-like vine seemed to open up more cuts on his hands. What did it matter? His hands hurt, they were damp with something, and if he fell, he'd die. He still needed to get to the top regardless of anything else.

Seb reached a ledge at the top and grabbed it, his hands on fire. After he'd pulled himself up, he looked down. His head spun and his stomach lurched. He stared at the hard ground, now about fifty metres below.

All of Seb's upper body ached from the ascent, but just before he could stop to rest, the gargantuan looked up. Its green eyes widened and it loosed another shrill scream, its mouth stretching into a dark pit filled with jagged teeth. The pitch of it hurt Seb's ears and he watched Gurt slip because of the sound. The Mandulu might have lost his legs, but he managed to hold onto the vine, scrabble for a second or two, and resume his climb.

Brown skin beneath its brown fur, the beast on Seb's tail snapped its large jaws and started to climb up behind him. Its powerful forearms made light work of the tough vine.

Gurt had nearly made it to the top by the time the monster on his tail twigged. It grabbed the vine Gurt was climbing and shook it, screaming as it did so. But Seb couldn't stay around to help him. Without any more delay, he ran off into the forest.

The trees were so dense it took for Seb to burst free of them to see the view. He stopped for a second and looked over the green canopy below. He currently stood on top of a mountain. The sound of bird songs called louder than ever, and he watched several multicoloured creatures fly above the trees. In front of him stood what could only be described as a natural water slide. Made from algae-coated rock, it seemed to be the only way down, or at least the quickest. The piercing call from the monsters on his tail got louder. The beasts would be on him soon. He sat down, the cool water soaking through his trousers and boxer shorts, and he pushed off.

As Seb hurtled down the chute—his stomach in his throat —his world slowed down. Good job, really, because every few seconds he had to either duck or dodge a protruding root or rock. The splash of the water made it trickier, the spray nearly blinding him. He had to shield his eyes as he tried to avoid the natural hazards.

The chute straightened out, so Seb looked behind him to see first Gurt and then both monsters sliding down after him.

A large rush of water smothered Seb when he turned back around again, forcing a lungful of it down his throat. As he choked, a loud *thoom* ran through his skull, his ears rang, and stars sparkled in his vision. Dizzy and out of control, the root hadn't quite knocked him out, but it had come close. Before he could manage his recovery, the chute disappeared from beneath him.

Weightless, Seb flew through the air. His arms and legs windmilled as he looked down at the turquoise pool below him and prepared for the impact with the water. With everything slowed down, he braced himself in anticipation of the inevitable pain.

When he hit the warm pool, the water stung, each agonising second of it dragged out longer because of his ability.

A second later Gurt flew from the bottom of the chute. Seb's world had returned to normal speed again and he winced to see the brute bellyflop into the body of water with a loud slap. Gurt fell instantly limp as he sank beneath the surface.

Seb dived under and swam down to the Mandulu. He grabbed the dumb—and now limp—creature by his collar and pulled him to safety.

The pool got shallow enough near the edge for Seb to stand up. The cool water offered some relief to his cut hands, and with a tight grip still on Gurt's collar, he managed to drag him to the water's edge before letting go.

Instead of gratitude, malice twisted Gurt's features. "Why did you just save me? I was doing all right on my own."

Although what did Seb expect? The human race had an ego that often got them into trouble, but the Mandulus' ego eclipsed anything he'd seen from even his own species. Not only had Gurt been rescued, but he'd been rescued by someone who had no damn right rescuing him.

Even in his exhausted state, Seb smiled at the large creature. He then winked, blew him a kiss, and looked up to see the two huge monsters fly through the air as they exited the water chute one after the other. For the briefest moment they blocked out the sun. "I'd worry more about them than me if I were you."

Before Gurt could reply, Seb sprinted off into the thick undergrowth of the jungle.

CHAPTER 11

Seb ran through the thick jungle, jumping moss-covered rocks and ducking low-lying branches. Now he'd gotten more into the heart of the lush landscape, the sound of tropical birds set the air alight with their chorus. The brief spell of coolness from the water chute had now turned into a gushing sweat, his skin as moist as it had been when he stepped out of the pool.

The humidity beneath the thick jungle canopy hung twice as heavy in the air, making it hard to breathe, but Seb fought against his body's inability to cope with his surroundings and forced himself forwards. Although he heard the splashing of water behind him from either Gurt or the monsters, he'd got far enough away that he couldn't see the azure pool anymore.

Seb might have managed to avoid the bulky parts of nature that stood in his way, but smaller branches, vines, and leaves smacked into him as he ran. Each one seemed to cause their own light scratch and open up fresh wounds for his salty sweat to run into.

When one particularly large leaf slapped Seb in the face and caught his eye, his vision blurred. Although tempted to stop, he pushed on. He had a lead over the predators behind him that he didn't want to concede.

Seb's sight cleared and he stopped dead, halting himself just before he reached the edge of a cliff. To look down made his stomach lurch; the rocky ground below would make light work of a fragile human body. When he looked above him, he saw two metal tracks spanned the gap like an inverted monorail. A deep breath to try to still his furious heartbeat and he reached up.

The ground shook as the creatures pursuing him got closer, the snap and crack of twigs and trees responding to their heavy charge. The pair sounded like a demolition crew moving through the jungle, but Seb still couldn't see them or Gurt when he looked behind.

A small device hung down from the track. Seb currently had a loose grip on the handles. It looked like a bike for his hands. Without any further pause, he tightened his stinging and sweaty grip, pulled his legs up so he hung in mid-air, and pedaled with everything he had.

"Don't look down," Seb said to himself as he turned the device forward, the smell of grease coming from the inverted bike's movement. Racked with tiredness and his hands greasy, if he looked down now, it would only guarantee that he'd slip.

Seb's upper body screamed at him as if the muscles tore with every rotation. Scaling the vine had already taken the strength from him, and now this weird bike thing seemed like it could finish him off.

With clenched teeth and pain tearing through his muscles, Seb screamed as he willed himself through every turn. Each full cycle moved slower and more stuttered than the last.

When the entire track shifted, Seb looked behind to see the brown beast had the metal track in its grip and it looked determined to rip it down. Gurt had traveled about halfway across the track next to him and his beast also seemed more concerned with encouraging Gurt to fall than with catching up to him. It banged its heavy fists against the rail and roared thunder.

Just a few metres to go and Seb dug deep as he continued to turn the handles of the device. Every muscle ached and bile burned in his throat.

At the other side, Seb jumped from the upside-down bike, fell to his knees, and vomited into the lush green undergrowth. Were it not for the creature behind him, he would have stayed there. But the beast followed him over, swinging like an ape as it moved hand over hand to get across the crevice.

A few seconds passed where Seb watched the brute, its stubby black legs swaying as it came after him. It snapped its sharp teeth as if it could taste the air between them.

Seb clambered to his feet again and stumbled off in the direction of the pit.

WHEN SEB SAW A LADDER, HE LOOKED UP TO SEE THE TOP OF it and shook his head. Nothing had been this easy so far; this ladder surely had more to it than he could currently see. Although the fact that there was only one, and two people needed to escape …

Seb stretched his mouth wide while he ran to pull as much air into his tight lungs as he could. He'd easily get there before Gurt.

Having lost sight of the beast chasing him again, Seb still heard it as it closed the distance between them. With arms of jelly, he used his legs to climb the rungs.

At the top of the ladder, Seb stumbled and fell forward. Finally out of the undergrowth, he found himself on a hot black rock. The ledge stood about as high as the mountain he'd climbed previously and felt hot enough against his sweating face to fry an egg on.

Seb got to his feet and paused to recover. The treetops spread away from him as a carpet of green and he saw the birds he'd heard as they circled above the jungle. Were it not for the roars behind him, he would have stayed longer. A glance behind to where he'd come from and the back of his knees tingled. He'd been so occupied with his escape, he didn't appreciate just how high he'd climbed. He then saw Gurt reach the ladder and scale it. A few seconds later, the two beasts burst from the dense jungle. Thick saliva fell from their gnashing teeth, and when they looked up, a single-minded intent glowed in their green eyes.

Seb turned his back on the trio again to see the pit jutting from the canopy like a jagged tooth. They'd nearly made it. Although, how he'd fight when he got there … "One thing at a time, Seb," he muttered to himself.

Two zip wires had been set up side by side. They led back into the deep green lushness of the jungle ahead. Not that Seb wanted to return to the claustrophobic tightness of the over-grown space, but what other choice did he have?

If Gurt had gotten to the zip wires first, would he have sent them both down at the same time? Would he have left Seb stranded with the beasts on the rock plateau? Whatever Gurt would do didn't matter. As much as he hated the crea-ture, they would meet in the pits. Seb would finish him off without having to cheat.

The hanging bike had killed Seb's upper body, but he'd managed to get some of his strength back. He wrapped as tight a grip as he could around the zip wire's handlebars and, with one final breath, he fell forward. The metal cable whooshed as he hurtled back down into the dense forest, the wind billowing in his ears and tossing his hair.

Seb expected a soft landing, maybe even water. So when he broke the canopy and saw the rocky ground, panic ran ice through his veins. The crash sent him flying and ran a jarring pain through both of his knees. It felt like shards of glass had been wedged beneath his patellas.

Sprawled on the ground, Seb thought about staying there. Maybe he should just let the beasts win.

But he couldn't. Seb got to his feet again.

As Seb burst through into another clearing, he saw what he hoped to be the final obstacle: two long escalators instead of steps to the pit. One must have been for him and one for Gurt. They crossed a deep ravine. Although he hadn't looked around, it didn't take a genius to know the escalator would be the only path across to the other side.

Two heavy thuds shook the ground beneath Seb's feet. The creatures must have made it to the bottom of the zip wire.

The escalators ran quickly and in the wrong direction. Of course they did! One final deep breath into his weary body and Seb ran up the metal stairs.

The *tok tok tok* of Seb's feet against the steps seemed like a ticking bomb. The explosion would be the complete collapse of his body.

Seb heard what he assumed to be Gurt jump onto the escalator next to him; a second later he heard the heavy thuds of the creatures join them.

The hanging bike had drained him, but Seb found an extra gear and screamed as he pounded against the escalator. Just a few metres until the top, he jumped for it and grabbed a large rock as the metal stairs raked against his legs, threatening to drag him back down again.

Seb pulled himself to the top of the escalator, snatching his legs free from the moving stairs. Exhausted from the obstacle course, he looked up to see a large red button just a few metres from him.

On his feet again, wobbling from where his body threatened to give out beneath him, Seb stumbled to the button and slammed his hand down on top of it.

A loud foghorn sounded. The escalator Seb had just climbed broke apart and fell into the crevice below it, beast and all. He rested on the plinth the button sat on top of and looked at the second red button in front of Gurt's escalator. One press and he'd win. Moses hadn't given them any rules to follow.

Seb waited instead.

A few seconds later Seb saw Gurt. Red-faced and sweating, the huge Mandulu looked close to beaten.

"Come on, Gurt, you can do it. Just a few more steps."

Wincing, Gurt somehow managed to find the extra strength to get up the escalator. The beast that followed him ran just metres behind.

When Seb watched Gurt fall to the ground at the top, he looked at his red button. "If you don't get up soon, Gurt … You know what, never mind." He slapped Gurt's button and a second foghorn sounded.

Gurt's escalator broke apart, and just as the beast on Gurt's tail looked ready to leap forward, it fell back down with it.

Gurt first looked behind him and then back at Seb. The grimace of exhaustion turned into one of malice and Gurt raised one side of his mouth in a snarl, exposing his thick teeth. "I didn't ask you for your help." He got to his feet, breathing hard, but seemingly able to find more strength.

Gurt pointed behind Seb at the fighting pit. "Let's finish this," he said, his entire body moving with his laboured breaths.

Seb filled his lungs with a deep inhale of the humid air around them, wiped some of the sweat from his brow and nodded. "Okay."

CHAPTER 12

From a distance, the fighting pit seemed to stand tall and resolute. Although when Seb got closer to it, he saw how nature had attacked the vast stone structure. Vines and branches grew along and through it. What should have been the smooth surface of a finely constructed pit had lumps and bumps from where nature's inevitable growth had forced some of the huge stones out from the wall.

In spite of entropy, the pit remained an imposing sight. It still stood tall enough to block out the sun when the pair got close. Its shadow lay as a vast pool on the lush ground and offered enough shade to grant a welcome relief from the sweltering jungle.

The pair stared straight ahead as they strode side by side. Seb had never walked into an arena this way before. Usually his opponent either entered the ring from the opposite side or would be there waiting for him already.

The sun hid behind the pit, which allowed Seb to look up at the top of its walls without being dazzled. They had a jagged finish to them from the large rocks of the structure having crumbled away and fallen to the ground. They'd dropped so long ago, most of them now existed as moss-covered lumps. The rough top of the structure made him look across at the broken horns of his opponent. Both had the same craggy finish to them.

The only sound the pair made came from the crunch of the brush beneath their feet.

A large tunnel—big enough to ride a horse and cart through—gave them access to the ancient arena. Maybe in the old days they'd done chariot racing inside it too; it certainly had the space for it.

The pair's footsteps echoed in the tight tunnel and Seb noticed the slight irregularity of Gurt's stride. Since he'd become aware of the Mandulu's limp, he couldn't ignore it. Not that he would mention it to him, regardless of how tempted he felt to do so.

The lush greenery gave way to a sandy floor, which the strong wind picked up and threw at the pair. It stuck to Seb's sweating skin and burned his eyes. It clogged his nostrils—dampening his sense of smell—and dried his mouth. Every time he clenched his jaw, the pop of grit snapped through his skull.

When Seb stepped into the arena, he gasped and his mouth fell wide. The sun hung high in the sky, beaming down through the open roof like a spotlight. The ancients on many planets had treated their suns like gods. Most buildings of importance incorporated them into their designs.

With the heat soaking into his already sweating skin—the humidity slightly eased because of the dust surrounding him —Seb spun on the spot and looked up at the seats that would have once been packed with spectators. They currently sat empty, but he could almost hear the raucous crowd calling and jeering in anticipation of the fight. In its day, the pit must have been a sight to behold. He'd never been in one as large.

Four huge towers stood around the edge of the arena. Although the pit had been circular in its design, they gave the space corners. At least, they used to. Now just two remained fully erected while the other two stood half-formed, snapped off like broken and craggy twigs.

A deep inhale caused Seb's nostrils to clog with even more sand. Another heavy gust of wind ran through the place, tossing his hair back, cooling the sweat on his body, and throwing another wave of grit at him. He covered his eyes with his forearm and felt the sandblast against his skin.

The pair's near-silent journey culminated with them arriving in the middle of the arena, and Seb turned to the Mandulu beside him. For a moment he looked at the brute and his dark scowl. "Are you sure you want to do this?"

The response came back as a phlegmy growl. "Don't flatter yourself, human. You won't last two seconds."

Hard to suppress his smile, Seb shrugged. In some way, the grandeur of the place had given him a boost. It felt almost as if the spirits of warriors from a bygone age walked into the arena with him. Where he'd been drained from the assault course, he now felt ready to go again. "I'll see if I can break a bit more off those damaged horns, shall I? Leave something to remember me by long after I knock you out."

The right side of Gurt's leathered lip lifted.

Seb dropped into his fighting stance, stepped a few paces away, and raised his fists.

"Three," Seb said and Gurt tensed up as he too readied himself for the fight.

"Two." The pair stared at one another, Gurt's red eyes on fire with rage and resentment. He knew Seb had saved him on the obstacle course and, knowing Gurt, he'd want to reclaim his pride.

"One." As always, Seb's world slipped into slow motion

and he watched the large Mandulu rush him. The limp he'd heard in the tunnel now stood out as a weak spot on Gurt's thick frame. His right knee and his chin; both would drop him to the dusty ground if hit hard enough. Not that he would go for the knee. He only needed to beat him, not cripple him. Maybe if Gurt had been a fighter, his bad knee would be a problem for future missions, but he'd been put on the team because of his aim. So deadly with a blaster, Gurt's knee wouldn't come into question when he got deployed in the field.

The heavy beat of Gurt's footsteps ran through the dusty ground. Nothing compared to the monsters that had chased them in the jungle, but enough to remind Seb that the brute closing in on him weighed easily twice as much as he did. No doubt one of his punches would reflect that.

Seb stepped to one side and avoided Gurt's wild swing. The beast's large fist flew past his face, dragging a gust of wind with it as it nearly scraped his nose. One thing he'd learned the hard way; if he got hit when his world had slowed down, it still bloody hurt.

After Seb's successful evasion, he watched Gurt stumble past him, his face scrunched up with the rage he'd tried to channel into his punch. He cuffed the brute around the back of the head. He might have decided to go easy on Gurt's knee, but that didn't mean he'd miss the opportunity to humiliate him.

Gurt spun around—his wide frame hunched, his fat jaw hanging open with his ragged breaths—and Seb winked at him. "Come on, sweetheart, you can do better than that."

Gurt screamed and rushed at Seb again.

It played out in the same way as before; Seb avoided Gurt's swing and clipped him around the back of his head on his way past.

The second time Gurt turned to face him, Seb laughed. "Where's the warrior you'd pretended to be? I thought you knew how to fight?"

Gurt rushed forward, but this time he didn't get as far as Seb. Instead he collided with what seemed to be an invisible barrier between them. A loud *tonk* sounded and he fell backwards, landing on his arse on the dusty ground.

Seb put his hands out in front of him. When he felt the barrier, he pushed against it. It stood cold and resolute like a thick sheet of reinforced glass. "What the …?"

The impact seemed to have dazed Gurt, who lay on the ground, holding his head. Although Seb took a breath to speak, words flashed up on the barrier between them. They read YOU NEED TO GO OUTSIDE THE PIT TO FINISH THIS BATTLE.

Gurt must have received the same message, because he went from being dazed to getting to his feet and sprinting off toward the exit on his side of the arena. He seemed to realise he'd been given a lifeline.

CHAPTER 13

Seb followed Gurt's lead and sprinted off in the opposite direction to the limping Mandulu. An exit on both sides of the pit—and a seemingly immovable barrier between them —he had to go back the way he'd come from.

The world had returned to normal speed and the hard ground ran shocks up Seb's body as his tiredness flooded back into his system. Adrenaline from entering the pit had spurred him on, but now the opportunity to fight had passed, his fatigue returned with a vengeance. Had he not been such an egotistical prick more focused on humiliating Gurt than beating him, then he could have knocked the Mandulu out cold in the arena and he wouldn't have to deal with this crap.

The slap of Seb's clumsy feet echoed in the tunnel as he ran back through it. The wind whipped across the front of the space, sending out a deep and continuous tone like someone blowing across the top of a large bottle. When he burst out into the vibrancy of the jungle, he stopped dead.

As Seb stared at the small ship in front of him, he shook his head. Sparks flew the ships, not him. All the time he'd had to end Gurt, and it came to this. A battle in a thing he couldn't even pilot.

Robbed of his motivation, Seb trudged toward the ship.

Once in the cockpit, Seb sat in the padded pilot's seat. It smelled of leather and had been made from the hide of a hairy yellow-skinned creature. He looked at the console, hoping to be struck by inspiration. Nothing. An array of buttons—all of them in different shapes and sizes—Seb didn't have the first clue on which one to press.

Lost as he stared at the cockpit, Seb reached out to touch one of the buttons but stopped dead when he looked out of the windscreen. A ship, identical to the one he occupied, hovered above him, its engines whining. Close enough for him to see the broken-tusked grin of the Mandulu in the cockpit, he muttered, "Damnit," as two thick red beams hurtled toward him.

Seeing the world in normal speed, Seb barely drew a breath before the beams connected with his ship and white light exploded around him.

THE BRIGHT FLASH OF THE EXPLOSION MORPHED INTO THE stark and clinical glare of the simulator room as the pair were pulled from their virtual confrontation. Numb and exhausted from the experience, Seb looked across at Gurt, who stood panting as he stared out of the glass room at the spectators.

Now Seb had been dragged from the illusion, he remembered the crowd that had watched him go in. It seemed to have doubled in size. It looked like everyone in the complex had found their way there. All of them would have seen him toying with Gurt in the arena. An arrogant prick, he could have knocked him out and been done with it. Instead—

The hard pats on Seb's back knocked him forward a step. When he turned to look at his smug opponent, he muttered, "Well done."

A broad grin pushed Gurt's large chin forward. "It was rather, wasn't it? And for a moment I thought you might have had me beat in the arena."

The victor always wrote history. No matter what had happened during the simulation, Seb had lost. Maybe he shouldn't have pressed the button to drop Gurt's bridge. Maybe he should have banged him out cold in the arena. Maybe he should have loosed his zip wire when he had the chance. Maybe he should have done a lot of things. But instead, he behaved like a moron because of his overinflated confidence. And now—in front of the entire complex—his pride had to pay the price.

After he'd watched Gurt leave the simulation room to be surrounded by many of the spectators, Seb walked out after him. SA remained in the crowd and watched him instead of Gurt. Her eyebrows lifted in the middle, almost like she felt sorry for him. Either that, or she'd been genuinely confused by his actions.

Before Seb could look at her any longer, Moses stepped in front of him. For a moment, the two stared at one another before Moses spoke. "You could have finished that several times. Don't show your enemies the same kindness. There are no rules in war. You need to remember that."

Shame set fire to Seb's face and he didn't reply. Once Moses had walked off, Seb looked at the ground and headed back to his room.

CHAPTER 14

"So why didn't you just knock him out?" Sparks asked as they walked toward the canteen.

Seb involuntarily ground his jaw in reaction to Sparks' question. Sure, it seemed like an obvious thing to ask him; after all, he did have Gurt at his mercy in the arena. Had he sparked him, then everything would have been settled. The click of his and Sparks' heels fell into line together. The sound bounced off the hard steel walls of the corridor, highlighting his refusal to respond.

"I mean, we could all see you were toying with him, but …"

"Did SA see that? Oh, my god, I must have looked like such a prat."

When Sparks didn't reply, Seb looked at her to see she had an eyebrow raised at him. "I think it would take a bit more than that for her to think of you as an idiot."

"She said something?" Seb instantly flushed hot. "I mean … um."

Sparks' shrill laugh echoed through the corridor. "Of

course she hasn't *said* anything. She doesn't speak, remember?"

Seb looked at the canteen instead of Sparks. If his face looked like it felt, it currently glowed like a beacon.

The second Seb entered the room, the place fell quiet. So quiet he could hear his own pulse. The small few who hadn't watched the simulation would have heard about it by now.

Seb's stomach twisted and his pulse sped up as he walked past Gurt's table. The vulgar creature sat surrounded by syco-phants, members of his own species, and SA. To look at her made him want to crawl into a hole and hide with the shame of his own foolhardiness.

SA didn't smile, but she didn't look at Seb with contempt either. Impartial, she silently observed him. He sighed as he took in her long blonde hair, her yellow skin, her iridescent blue gaze. He'd been such a fool.

After Seb had passed Gurt and his harem, his shoulders snapped to his neck to hear the large creature's voice. "You could have finished me, you know?"

Seb stopped, but he didn't turn around.

"You had me beat. You could have dropped my escalator into the crevice, but you didn't. I don't think you have what it takes."

And maybe he didn't. Gurt didn't mention that he'd had him beat in the pit. Seb could tell him that he knew about his weak knee and he went easy on him, but he wouldn't stoop to Gurt's level. He'd made a choice to behave like an idiot once already, he didn't need to do it again.

A long-fingered hand rested against Seb's back and Sparks spoke so only he could hear. "Come on, let's go and get some lunch."

"I don't feel very hungry," Seb whispered to her.

"Don't let him get to you. It's not worth it."

That much seemed obvious, but Gurt had burrowed into Seb like a tick, and he couldn't get the vile creature out.

Before Seb moved off, Gurt laughed and said, "I think you're a little mummy's boy. You should go home and suck on her teat some more."

Although Seb felt Sparks try to grab him, he got away from her as he dashed over toward Gurt. One step on an empty seat on the other side of the table from the large beast, and he launched himself at him. As he flew through the air, everything slowed down and he saw SA's mouth fall open in shock.

Gurt flinched and raised his arms, but Seb knocked his defence aside and grabbed the Mandulu's thick throat. His momentum knocked Gurt backwards off his seat, and the pair of them fell to the hard floor. Gurt bore the brunt of the landing as the empty chairs around them scattered and fell over.

Seb clenched his teeth so hard they ached. He raised his fist, saliva dribbling from his mouth as he drove his hand at Gurt's bulbous chin. But before he could make contact, his arm stopped. When he looked up, he found Moses over him, every tooth in his wide mouth bared in a fierce warning. The world returned to normal speed and for the first time in what felt like forever, Seb backed down from a fight.

If it had been silent when Seb entered the canteen with Sparks, the lack of sound in the place had now turned it into a vacuum.

Moses shouted, the bass note of his voice blurring Seb's vision and upsetting his balance. "Get off him *now*!"

Seb did as ordered, his breathing heavy from the exertion as he stood up and faced Moses.

With a thick finger, Moses pointed at Gurt, SA, and

Sparks. "You, you, and you, I have a mission for you. Come with me."

Instead of telling Seb to join them, Moses lifted him clean from the ground by the back of his shirt.

Seb couldn't breathe and stars swam in his vision. Before he could pull at his collar to try to free his airways, Moses threw him in the direction of the canteen's exit. Seb walked with his shoulders slumped and his head dropped. One day he and Moses would fall out. Then he would take back the pride the large man had just stripped from him.

CHAPTER 15

Moses held the door open for the four of them. Seb watched the three others enter before he did. SA led the line. She moved with her usual grace and confidence and walked into the place like she'd chosen to be there.

Gurt—oblivious to much other than himself and things that needed to be killed—lumbered in next.

Sparks' eyes darted around the place, and maybe Seb was the only one to know why. He watched her look at every electrical device and power point. It gave her the edge should anything go wrong.

Seb followed them in to the bland room, the air conditioning cold enough to pull his skin tight, but not quite give him goosebumps.

Most of the lights were off and a row of seats had been laid out at the front. A monitor took up an entire wall. The only illumination came from small white spotlights embedded in the floor to highlight the path through the room, not that anyone other than a moron needed the guidance. Predictably, Gurt watched the floor as he walked.

The space reminded Seb of the cinemas he'd visited back on Danu, sans the reek of sweet food, child sick, and sweat.

Following the others' leads, Seb sat down. When the only seat happened to be next to SA, he would have been rude to ignore it. Despite their path through training together, he hadn't gotten close to her often, and to be next to her now, their shoulders close to touching, elevated his heart rate just enough to make him giddy. She smelled of sweet flowers. She smelled of summer on a planet he hadn't yet visited, but one he could fall in love with when he found it.

It took for Gurt to look across, stare down at Seb's right leg, and let out a low growl for him to realise he sat there with his leg bouncing. The excitement of sitting next to SA did strange things to him. He looked straight back at the large beast and made a point to bounce it more.

Before Gurt could react, Moses slammed the door, the shock of the loud bang forcing Seb to jump in his seat. The shark-like creature stomped down to the front of the room and pointed at Seb and Gurt. "I'm getting sick of the nonsense going on between you two. You're about to go on a mission together, so you need to start working as a team. Whatever petty squabble you're having, it ends now, got it?"

Seb drew a breath to reply, but Moses cut him short. "Don't answer that. I'm not asking for your compliance; I'm giving you an order."

The entire room lit up from the glow of the large screen when Moses waved his hand in front of it. It showed an image of what looked like a planet. The place seemed dark, like they'd captured the footage of it at night. Moses moved his hands to drag the representation from the screen and hold it in mid-air.

After he'd spun the image, he stopped it and pointed to a built-up part of what otherwise looked like a sparse planet.

"This is the planet Solsans and its only city, Caloon." Moses zoomed in on the built-up rendering of Caloon. "As you can see, the city has two distinct parts to it." A large part of Caloon poked up from the ground, elevated from the rest of the dwellings surrounding it. Moses pointed at that part first. "This is the wealthy area of the city. The Crimson Countess' palace is here. Residents with enough credits in their bank live on this elevated patch of land.

"And this," Moses said as he pinched the air to go close in on the dwellings around the bottom, "is where the poor people live. The city is divided between the haves and the have-nots."

As if scrunching up a ball of paper, Moses crushed the image in front of him and threw it back at the screen. This time, he used wider hands than before to pull a broader view of Solsans out in front of him. He tapped it so it spun on the spot and showed more of the rural area surrounding the city. "The rest of Solsans is covered in rocky mountains and thick woodland. It's where a lot of the mines are, but most people don't go away from the city because of the hostile landscape."

When Seb felt Gurt lean forward next to him, he watched the large beast address Moses. "So why are you showing us this?"

His already broad chest puffed out further as Moses straightened his back with a deep inhale. "For the good of my health. Why do you think, you moron? You have a mission here."

'Moron' didn't sit well with Gurt, and Seb couldn't help but smile to see him rest back in his seat, his bulbous jaw tight as he clenched it.

Like SA and Sparks further down the line, Seb kept his mouth shut and waited for Moses to explain.

"This is a search and rescue mission." A tap in mid-air brought up the photo of a slightly podgy man with floppy hair. "This is George Camoron." Moses seemed to take great pleasure in enunciating the 'moron' part of his name. "He's got himself kidnapped by the Crimson Countess. His daddy, a rich tycoon who got to the top by screwing over anyone and everyone who got in his way, runs a commodity company. He owns a planet called Debula. Have you heard of them?"

"They're the former politicians turned miners, right?" Sparks said.

Moses nodded.

"They use their old political connections to find out which planets have resources worth stealing, go to those planets with the promise of employment and stabilisation, bleed them dry of every commodity they own, and then leave them bereft and unable to support their inflated economy that existed while the mining took place. They're the galaxy's parasites."

A genuine smile split Moses' face. "Someone knows their stuff. Obviously, with Debula now being our client, I'd advise holding some of those views back at the risk of causing offence."

Sparks nodded.

"So little George went to Solsans hoping to check out the validity of setting up operations there. As you can imagine, the Crimson Countess didn't take kindly to that. She captured and imprisoned him. George should have gone in on a covert mission, but it would seem that Camoron's influence in certain parts of the galaxy had gone to his head. He thought he could knock on their front door and put the proposal to them."

Seb looked down the line to his left when Sparks spoke again. "So why are we rescuing this vile creature? Surely he deserves everything he gets."

Another scrunching motion to take the red-faced fop from the screen and Moses grinned, revealing his sharp teeth. "Because Daddy has a lot of money. A lot of money he's prepared to pay to get young George back."

The next image showed what seemed to be a female figure. She stood tall and was cloaked in red. "This is the Crimson Countess."

"Why can't we see her face?" Seb asked as he stared at the darkness inside her hood.

"Very few people have seen it," Moses explained. "A very secretive woman, it takes a lot to get close enough to get her picture."

The recycled air left a stale taste on Seb's tongue. The image of the woman seemed to bring the bad taste to the foreground of his mouth.

"Camoron has been there for a few years. The reason we're only going on a rescue mission now is because the Camorons have sent this to me." Moses fished a small plastic device from his pocket and held it up in a pinch.

"A memory stick," Sparks said.

"It certainly looks that way," Moses replied. "But I can't be sure because we can't access it."

When he showed Sparks the connector on the end of it, her purple eyes narrowed, crushed by her frown. "What the …"

"I know, right?"

Seb glanced at SA and Gurt. They looked as confused as he felt.

Moses turned the memory stick to show the rest of the room. "This connecter is alien to us. To break into the stick to retrieve the data could corrupt it. Our best guess is that the systems on Solsans use these ports on their machines."

The chair groaned beneath Gurt's girth as he leaned

toward Moses again. "So we've got to go and find a computer to access it? What's supposed to be on there that's so special?"

"The information for the whereabouts of every prisoner on Solsans," Moses said, "including Camoron. The Camorons had to pay handsomely for this little stick. The smuggler who brought it off Solsans can never go back for fear of a run-in with the Countess.

Something about the mission sank cold dread through Seb, and when he looked to his left and right, it would appear that his colleagues felt it too. Well, SA looked her usual serene self, but the other two wore heavy frowns of concern.

"Now," Moses said with a clap of his hands that cracked so loud it made Seb's ears ring, "go back to your rooms and get everything you need. We're leaving for Solsans in two hours' time."

CHAPTER 16

S eb and Sparks had left their cube of a room set up as a bedroom. So when they returned to the small space, Seb climbed up to the top bunk and lay down.

Whenever they left the room unoccupied, the temperature quickly dropped, but before Seb could say anything, he looked over to see Sparks adjust the thermostat in the panel of buttons on the wall. She clicked it up to twenty-four degrees Celsius and pressed the button next to it labeled *boost*. Within seconds, the room's temperature rose to the one specified, encouraging him to relax into his pillow.

A dull throb ran down Seb's shin from attacking Gurt earlier. He must have clattered into something on his way over the tables.

The heat of the room combined with his exhaustion turned Seb's body to lead and he sank into his mattress. He continued to watch Sparks, who paced the room with her screen in her hand. The glow from the tiny device lit up her face and reflected off her glasses. As he watched her, his eyelids grew heavy.

"What are you doing?"

Seb woke with a start, his eyes burning and his vision blurred. "Huh?"

"What are you doing? We need to get ready to go to Solsans."

Seb blinked repeatedly to try to banish the sting in his tired eyes. "You might be getting ready to go, but I ain't. Moses doesn't own me. What if I object?"

"We've been through this already. If you object, you go to prison."

Although Sparks had spoken to him, she hadn't taken her eyes off her screen as she walked around the room and gathered up a small bag of things. Without looking, she filled her rucksack with cables and wires.

"This is bullshit," Seb said.

Sparks finally looked up at him.

"We have to risk our lives on some planet in the arse end of nowhere to save some clueless rich imbecile who deserves to be locked up anyway."

"There's a lot of assumptions there."

"Come on, Sparks, Moses told us the guy went there to see if he could mine the planet for their resources. You said their company bleeds planets dry and then leaves them decimated. Can you seriously tell me you want to do this?"

"Of course not, but we don't have a choice."

"There's *always* a choice."

"Yeah, prison or mission. And let me tell you, prison doesn't pay." Sparks continued to look at Seb, one of her hands on her hip and her eyebrow cocked. "Look, you know as well as I do that we're going on this mission because Daddy has a lot of money, and he'll pay anything to get his little darling back. But if you knew what the Crimson Countess was like, I think you'd want to go regardless. Now don't get me wrong, she scares me more than almost anything else scares me—"

"More than fire?"

"I said *almost*. But this woman needs to be stopped."

Sparks crossed the room and held her small computer up for Seb to see. Images flashed across the screen. It showed the slums of Caloon that Moses had shown them—the dwellings that surrounded the rich and elevated part of the city. They lay at the feet of the wealthy's raised plateau like followers prostrate in the shadow of a deity. "These people live like rats while the Crimson Countess and the others in the elevated city lord it over them. This isn't pretty, but watch." Sparks then played a video for him.

An army of soldiers, who all wore red robes, appeared on the screen and ran into the slum. The stamp of their feet beat against the ground in time like the fast beat of an execution-er's drum. "They're the Crimson foot soldiers, the Countess' army." The screen then suddenly lit up with a rush of fire and a loud *whoosh* sounded out. Thirty to fifty soldiers in total, they used flamethrowers to set fire to the tightly packed buildings in the slums.

A few seconds after the soldiers had torched the place, creatures of all shapes and sizes ran from their huts, screaming and crying. Ablaze like their properties, they fled the soldiers, but when they got a certain distance away, another line of the robed army held shields up at them and forced them back. The soldiers with the shields closed in from every side and drove them into the ones with the flamethrowers, who continued to set fire to everything.

The chaos of it sent Seb's mind reeling as he watched the innocent creatures burn. Some even cradled smaller versions of themselves in their arms. The cries of the newborns became the only decipherable noise in the bedlam. A shrill expression of pure agony. Fire didn't discriminate or show mercy; if you stood in its way, you burned. A glance at Sparks and Seb saw her wincing at the footage.

Then, as quickly as it had started, it ended. The video jumped forward in time. Where there had been bright orange flame, there now lay smoking huts and charred husks. In the short space of time, the skin of every creature—regardless of the colour before—had turned black and—depending on the colour of their blood—had lightning bolts of pink or green or blue streaked through them. Such vivid images, Seb could almost smell the burn of their flesh.

After Sparks lowered her computer, Seb looked at her, breathless and at a loss for words.

"That massacre happened because one person in that area of the slum stole a clean set of warm clothes. They caught him and decided to punish anyone who may have known him. This isn't an isolated incident." Sparks raised the mini-computer at Seb. "I can show you more if you like?"

Seb briskly shook his head. "No, thanks."

"I'm with you on the whole George Camoron thing," Sparks said. "The guy's a waste of oxygen. He's been preened and mollycoddled for his entire life and has no grip on reality, but that isn't why I'm going to Solsans. I'm going there to prove to the Crimson Countess that she doesn't have control over everything. That she can't do what the hell she likes. I'm going to rescue that rich imbecile just because we can, and if I get a chance to have a pop at her while I'm there, then I'm going to damn well take it."

The tiredness had left Seb and he sat up in his bunk. After he'd swung his legs over the side, he slipped off it and landed on the chrome floor of their room with a gentle thud. A nod to Sparks and he said, "Okay, you're right. We need to go there and try to do something about this demonic woman."

CHAPTER 17

The small ship rocked from side to side, tossed about by the snowstorm like a leaf in the wind. Seb stood up with Gurt, Sparks, and SA. They all held onto the railing that ran through the gunmetal grey vessel. To remain upright, Seb gripped the railing so hard it hurt his hand. Moses stood at the back of the ship, furthest away from the hatch that would open soon. Too soon.

The ship rocked and weaved in the extreme weather and Moses shouted to be heard by the recruits. "Sorry about the bumpy ride, but this is the only way onto Solsans. We need to get in and drop you off unnoticed if you're to stand any chance of completing this mission."

The shark-like creature's words sent a buzz of anxiety through Seb's guts. *Stand any chance* seemed much less positive than anything he'd heard before that. Not that he could do anything about it now. A deep breath did little to help, so he busied himself with getting dressed one-handed. He slipped on a thick coat and trousers like the others were, ready to face the snowy conditions below them.

The craft lurched sharply to the side and everyone went

with it. Although Seb remained anchored to the rail, the muscles in his arms ached to maintain his position.

Zero emotion sat in Moses' black glare when he continued to address the recruits. "There's a lot riding on this mission. We complete it successfully and the Shadow Order will be okay for cash flow for some time."

"So don't cock it up," Gurt called at Seb, a smug grin lifting his wide face.

After he'd locked stares with the ugly creature, Gurt's broken tusks rising with his facetious smile, Seb glanced at Sparks and then SA. The same azure compassion looked at him as if urging him to ignore the big idiot that she'd had to partner up with.

The coldness of Solsans' atmosphere worked its way through the gaps in the ship, and Seb's exposed hands stung as they turned numb. Clumsy with his diminishing lack of feeling, he grabbed his coat's zip in a pinch, did it up, and gripped the rail again. He then slipped his gloves on one at a time, using his teeth for the second glove.

Once he'd gotten himself ready, Seb looked at the others. Sparks checked her rucksack full of wires and devices. Gurt kept his coat open as he stuffed an unreasonable number of blasters inside, strapping them, it seemed, to every spare inch of his body. SA sharpened her knives, which seemed to be a favourite pastime of hers, and slipped them into her complex leather harness, which held more than seemed possible.

As if seeing his insecurities, Gurt nodded at Seb. "That's all you've got, is it? Your own two fists and your not so sharp wit?"

Moses spoke before Seb could respond. "We're going to drop you on the highest peak on Solsans so you can get into Caloon unnoticed. You'll need to use these"—he held up four snowboards and slid them along the ship to each member of the team—"to get down the mountain. At the bottom, you can dump all your gear."

"And how will we get off the planet again?" Seb had spoken without thinking, his directness leaving him open to criticism for insolence. But when the rest of the team, even Gurt, looked at Moses for an answer, he relaxed a little. At least they were united on that front.

The few seconds that Moses watched Seb for lasted an age before he said, "You get creative. We pay you guys because you come up with answers to problems. You'll work something out."

The four team members looked at one another.

Before anyone could say anything else, Moses shouted over the noise of the wind outside, "We're dropping you off in fifteen seconds. Get ready."

Seb had never been on a snowboard in his life. Maybe the others had, but he didn't have the first clue about using one.

"Ten seconds," Moses said as he pressed a button beside him.

The whir of the exit ramp on the ship sounded out. A second later an icy blast snapped Seb's body tight. He gripped onto the railing with all he had, his hair flapping in his eyes because of the strong breeze.

"Five seconds."

Gurt moved forward first, using both hands to pull himself along the railing above him toward the exit. His snowboard scratched against the ship's metal floor. Even the cocky Mandulu seemed to be questioning his courage as he looked out onto the mountain range below. They had about a five-metre drop to negotiate that could quite easily damage Gurt's knee.

"Go!" Moses called, and Gurt jumped.

SA followed a second later, launching herself from the

ship with her usual grace. She took to the air like a bird in flight.

Sparks followed them out and Seb looked over his shoulder at Moses one last time. A detached glare met him. A glare that offered no way out. A deep breath and he jumped from the ship, all of his attention on the snowy peak beneath him where his teammates had already landed with ease.

CHAPTER 18

I mmediately after touching down on the mountain, Seb plunged into a snowstorm. It restricted his visibility to just a few metres and the fresh snow crunched beneath his board as he raced over it. Unable to see the others, he called out, "Sparks?" but the wind grabbed his voice and obliterated it. With no other choice but to continue on, he pointed his board down the mountain and picked up speed.

After just a few seconds of what felt like maximum velocity, the snow smashing into his face and his ears on fire with the cold, Seb's world dropped into slow motion. It became much easier to see the dark grey rocks that jutted from the ground, and he managed to angle his body to avoid them. The starkness of his white surroundings enabled him to see the hazards.

Were it not for the slow motion, Seb wouldn't have made it. However, it made it so he felt the cold torture of every snowflake in the air as it hit him and then melted on his exposed skin. The cold had teeth, and after a short while, it felt as though nature had torn chunks from him.

The storm diminished as Seb got lower down the mountain, affording him a clearer view. The white expanse of the snowy slope lay before him. Three figures weaved in and out of one another and all three of them moved with a competence he could only dream of. Sparks, on a diminished board, zigzagged, hopped, and jumped, SA glided down the piste as if levitating, and Gurt cannoned toward Caloon like an avalanche. Seb only cared about remaining upright.

Now he'd left the clouds, Seb saw the dark city of Caloon below. Or rather, the elevated part of the city; the lower area sat hidden beneath a blanket of fog. It made the place seem impenetrable, but they'd find a way to complete their mission. They had to.

With his board pointing straight down, Seb caught up with the other three, receiving a long thumbs-up from Sparks, a smile from SA, and a look of utter contempt from Gurt. Despite the fierce concentration he needed to remain upright, he relaxed a little. At least he had his team around him.

Seb tried to slow himself down by snaking from side to side, his world still locked in slow motion. But instead of slowing down, he continued straight past the others as he gathered more momentum.

When he looked back up, he suddenly saw something that none of the others were aware of. Huge like elephants, they had brown fur, thick and powerful legs, and massive paws. Their faces were so crammed with teeth, it took him a second to see anything else in their gargantuan heads. They all had large red tongues that lolled from their drooling mouths. A herd of fifteen, maybe twenty, the huge bears gained on the other three as they ran down the slopes behind them.

Unable to slow himself down, Seb tried to shout at his team, but they couldn't hear him. He had to do something; otherwise he'd be arriving in Caloon on his own.

CHAPTER 19

One last look at the bears—the brown creatures galloping down the hill like hippos on the charge—and Seb wobbled on his board. The wobble turned into a snaking flick-flack and he went down. Even in slow motion, which gave him more of an ability to control his landing, the impact against the hard slope rattled his skeleton.

A sharp burn tore through Seb's shoulder when he hit the ground for a second time. He then smacked the side of his head against the slope. It rocked his world and sent stars flashing across his vision. The board remained attached to his feet as he rolled over and over.

By the time Seb stopped, his face stung from where he'd smashed into the snow. He looked up and watched Sparks, SA, and Gurt all flash past him. With the bears on their tail—all the more terrifying for his slow-motion perspective of them—he jumped up again and headed down the hill after the others.

Within seconds, the bears at the front of the pack caught up with Seb. One on his right opened its mouth so wide, he felt like he could be sucked into it. He'd certainly fit. The creature didn't have any visible weak spots, so he used the tail of his board to whack the beast's nose.

It knocked the large creature over, turning it into a ball of kicked-up snow and brown fur.

Another one replaced the beast, and when Seb looked down the mountain, not only did he see his team looking back up at him and his posse of bears, but he saw the huge rock that jutted from the pure white snow in the middle of the slope. With what little boarding skills he had, he edged toward the rock, turned to see the creature had all of its focus on him, and cut across the front of the large boulder at the last minute.

The creature yelped when it collided with the stone. It sounded like a puppy being kicked over a fence. All the more satisfying for the long, drawn-out slow motion Seb witnessed it in. Not that he had much time to enjoy it; three more of the beasts drew level with him, their heavy breaths and thundering paws coming on top of him like a landslide. Their hard respiration reeked of stale blood.

Before Seb could think, a red beam shot past him. It hit the bear closest to him directly between the eyes. Slowed down like everything else, he heard the squelch of it enter the creature's forehead, and then watched the explosion of blood, bone, and brains fly backwards away from the bear as it decorated the stark white snow behind it. The large brute fell and rolled sideways, tripping another one of its posse.

With a second to take his eyes from the beasts around him, Seb looked down the hill again. Sparks and SA had returned to their snaking paths, one on either side of Gurt, who boarded backwards, a blaster in each hand as he ripped off shots at the creatures.

The flurry of laser fire stood against the backdrop of the pitch-black night's sky. Every shot Gurt fired connected, and the bears went down one after the other. Yelp after yelp after yelp.

Seb's slow motion kept everything manageable as he weaved down the mountain, just out of the reach of the monsters on his tail. Snapping jaws full of teeth came close—too close for comfort—but none of them made contact.

The pack had been considerably thinned by Gurt's volley of laser fire, so just three of the beasts remained on Seb's tail. Maybe the most persistent. Maybe the ones with the best stamina. Maybe the slow ones who couldn't keep up but found themselves left by virtue of being the ones at the back.

Two laser shots ripped past Seb, one on each side of him. They ran so close they damn near tore the fabric of his jacket.

Not knowing if he should look at Gurt or the beasts he'd shot at, Seb watched the bears fall and then turned to the large Mandulu. A shake of his head and Gurt looked at the last bear on the slope.

When Seb looked behind, he saw the brute directly behind him. It made it impossible for Gurt to shoot him.

Seb moved left and the beast followed him. He moved right and so did the bear. With every metre they traveled down the mountain, the large animal gained on him.

A scan of his surroundings and Seb saw no sign of any rocks, trees, or any other obstructions he could encourage the bear to crash into.

Puffed out from avoiding the others, Seb felt the hot breath of the creature pushing against his back and the thud of its heavy footfalls through his board. When he looked down at his team, both Sparks and SA looked up, their jaws hanging loose, their eyes spread wide.

Gurt, however, pointed at the ground. How much did Seb trust the imbecile? He'd had no reason to before that point. The loud *snap* of the creature's jaws sounded closer than ever and Seb's heart backflipped. Another glance at Gurt and he saw him point at the ground again.

As if he were about to dive into an icy lake, Seb took one final deep breath and went down.

Like before, Seb hit the solid slope hard and spun over and over, the board still attached to his feet. Each impact against the compacted ground rattled through him, and as he rolled he caught glimpses of the brute behind him. It had leapt forward, its large paws—each one the size of his head—were outstretched in front of it. Like the first one that had caught up with him, this one seemed to have an abyss of a mouth that could consume him whole. Its rows of needle teeth would perforate him so he'd leak blood like a sponge leaking water.

But just before it landed on top of Seb, a red laser blast crashed into its nose, throwing the brute backwards. Its legs swung underneath it as the impact of the blast tossed the head of the beast away.

While still barreling down the hill and still moving in slow motion, Seb pushed up from the ground and got upright on his board again. A glance back the way they'd come from and he saw the mountainside strewn with the dead bodies of the bears. Blood soaked the white snow, and each brown lump of fur lay motionless.

CHAPTER 20

Seb caught up to the others at the bottom of the mountain. They'd stopped by the entrance to a cave.

The danger from the bears had passed, but Seb's world still moved in slow motion as he did his best to control the board strapped to his feet.

A glance at Sparks and SA, and then Seb looked at Gurt. He judged himself through the Mandulu's eyes for what he planned to do next, but he didn't have any other choice.

As Seb had already done a couple of times on the descent, he let himself fall over. He crashed into the snowy ground and rolled several times before he stopped at Gurt's feet.

The world returned to a normal speed for Seb as he looked up at his comrade, who shook his head at him. "You need to work on your boarding skills. What would you have done were I not there to save you?"

Although Seb opened his mouth to protest, Sparks stepped forward. "You don't get it, do you, Gurt?"

"Huh?"

"Seb went down on purpose."

A heavy scowl gripped Gurt's features. "Why would he do that?"

Still recovering from the run, Seb fought to get his breath back and stood up. Every slight movement ached his body. "You're right, Gurt, I don't know how to board. I needed to slow down enough to get behind you. It was the only way I could think of to get you guys to look up the mountain to see the monsters chasing you."

"So you purposefully went among them so we could see them?"

A look at SA and her brilliant gaze and Seb blushed before he let out a self-conscious laugh. "Um … yeah. It would have been a nasty surprise to be ambushed by that bunch, eh?"

Although Gurt looked like he had more to say, a grimace twisted his face and he remained quiet.

CHAPTER 21

After Seb detached his snowboard from his feet, he sought shelter inside the damp cave, rested his board against the wall, and removed his salopettes and ski jacket. He tossed them down on the black stone ground and inhaled the musty reek of the place.

No one spoke for a few seconds as the slow drip of melting snow played its wet metronome in the space. Seb stared down at his discarded items and broke the near silence. "I'm guessing we won't need this lot again."

A glance down at the equipment and Gurt raised an eyebrow. The Mandulu clearly still stung from Seb's purposeful falling over on the slopes. Or rather, his inability to see it where Sparks had. Other than general contempt, he had nothing to level at Seb at that moment and he seemed unsettled for it. He returned to removing his clothes and made a point to check that all of his blasters remained in place.

Sparks—who Seb had noticed watched Gurt like he had —shrugged and finally responded, "I hope not." After she'd tossed her board and clothes on top of Seb's, she put her rucksack on the ground, opened it up, and inspected the contents.

SA said nothing, as usual, but she also checked her equipment. Every razor-sharp knife caught the light and winked as she examined it. Like Gurt, she wore a leather harness that clung to her lithe form. It made the most practical use of the space to get as many knives on her person as she could physically carry. They were all strapped so tightly to her, she moved without a sound.

For the first time since the fight in the canteen with Gurt, Seb relaxed a little. With no equipment to check, he focused on his deep breaths as he tried to centre himself.

After a short while, Gurt seemed to be satisfied with the security of his blasters against his body and he turned his attention to Seb, as he often did when he got bored. "Why don't you have any equipment?"

At risk of sounding like a douche in front of SA, Seb raised his fists. "I don't need anything more than these." His fists and the ability he'd inherited from his mother. But Gurt didn't need to know that.

"How about some shooting practice?" Gurt suggested. The twinkle that sat in his red eyes whenever he tried to wind Seb up returned. Pleased with his own incredible wit, he flashed a facetious grin. "You could do with that."

But Seb didn't respond and Sparks stepped between them before it went any further. "Right, where do we go?"

"The fighting pits," Seb said.

The purple gaze of Sparks locked on Seb and she appraised him like she would an alcoholic asking to be taken to a bar. "Really?"

"As foreigners to this planet," Seb said, "the fighting pits are the one place I know where we won't stand out. They're always rammed with creatures from all over the galaxy. We go there and we can learn a lot about Caloon without raising suspicion."

An approving nod and Sparks looked at the other two. SA also nodded. Gurt remained silent. It wouldn't get any better than that from him.

Sparks had left her rucksack open, and when Seb saw a pair of binoculars on top of everything else, he leaned down, picked them up, and walked outside the cave.

Back out in the elements without his warm clothing, Seb tensed up against the frigid blast of nature. He clenched his jaw and shivered as he put the binoculars to his eyes. He looked out over the slum and elevated area of Caloon. Fog hung heavy in the air, but he could just about see the shapes of buildings through the green glow of night vision. When he saw the pit amongst the small raggedy huts that made up the slums, he pulled the binoculars away and handed them to Sparks.

Now Seb had seen it, the silhouette of the pit stood much clearer on the horizon for him. A huge colosseum of a place —as most of them were—he pointed for Sparks to see. "That has to be it."

Sparks handed the binoculars to Gurt, who used them before handing them to SA. When Seb took the binoculars back from SA, she held onto them a moment longer than he expected and the two looked at one another. A slow blink and she let go of them.

"I'm not a fan of this plan," Gurt said, bursting through the moment. "I mean, anything this rat says," he said while pointing at Seb, "I'm tempted to do the exact opposite of. There must be a better idea than this."

Seb looked at Gurt, as did Sparks and SA. None of them spoke. After a few seconds, Gurt sighed and his shoulders sagged. "Fine, if it goes wrong, don't say I didn't warn you."

Before either Seb or Sparks could reply, the sound of voices came at them from around the corner. As one, they all looked in the direction of the noise and withdrew back into the cave they'd just emerged from.

"We saw something on the radar," one of the voices said. A female voice, it sounded deep like it came from a creature of considerable size.

"It could just be some space junk," one of them replied. A male this time, his voice higher in pitch than the female's.

"But we have to check it out at least. Imagine if it *was* something and we didn't do anything about it. The Countess would skin us alive."

The last comment silenced the group. It seemed like the beings in the Countess' employ feared her like everyone else did.

The rustling of a bag pulled Seb's attention to the ground next to him. He saw Sparks rummaging through her things. When she stood up again, she had a small microphone plugged into her computer and she held it in the direction of the Crimson foot soldiers.

"Hey," one of the foot soldiers called out. "Look here! Footprints."

A deep breath to settle his rampaging heartbeat and Seb looked at the others. They didn't need words at that moment. From the looks on their faces, Seb could tell they all knew things were about to get hairy.

CHAPTER 22

The crunch of boots moved through the snow towards them and Seb edged closer to the cave's exit. Gurt and SA stepped forward with him, SA by his side, Gurt a little further back.

The moon cast enough light to throw the shadows of the foot soldiers across the snow. There must have been at least ten of them. Adrenaline pulled Seb's stomach tight and the edges of his world blurred as his gift kicked in.

When the first of the Crimson foot soldiers came into view, Seb couldn't identify its gender. Its face masked in shadow, it stood a little taller than him and a little wider. Not that gender mattered. When he saw the weak spot roughly where its nose should be, he lunged forward and drove a balled fist into it.

Before the foot soldier had a chance to look up, it crumpled beneath the blow, its legs folding under it. It sparked the battle to life.

Even when viewed in slow motion, SA moved like a tornado as she slipped out into the snow—a knife in each hand—and spun through the crowd of red robes.

All different shapes and sizes, the foot soldiers numbered far more than the ten Seb had anticipated. Forty or more, most of them had blasters and, after the initial shock of the ambush, they all drew their weapons. As SA worked through them—her long limbs fluid in her movement—the guards fired several shots in retaliation, all of which missed.

The weak spots of each creature stood out for Seb and he moved through the ones SA hadn't yet got to. Each one went down with a single blow as he avoided their sluggish attacks.

After he'd knocked out several of the brutes—his fists stinging from fighting in the cold—Seb caught sight of SA again. She moved with the poise of a ballerina, each graceful stroke controlled, seemingly choreographed for both beauty and deadly efficiency.

White light exploded through Seb's left eye and dragged him away from the mesmerising SA. He looked up to see a beast twice his size with fists like boulders. As he reeled from the blow, his world sped up.

The chaos of the battle surrounded Seb: screams, cries, blaster fire. Slow motion rendered sound meaningless, and although it didn't mute the battle, it stretched each noise out to the point where he didn't hear it.

At full speed, the cacophony of the fight made Seb dizzy, SA turned into a blur, and Gurt spawned pyrotechnics from his blasters. He didn't realise what Gurt could do until he saw him in real time. With his thick fingers working on the triggers, he released a constant stream of fire and every blast hit its mark.

A shake of his head and Seb returned to slow motion just in time to duck the next blow from the brute that had already hit him.

Seb's legs coiled like springs as he dropped down, fueling his leap to explode back up again and catch the monster on the chin. A wet *clap* as fist connected with jaw, and the beast's head snapped back. It stumbled for a second and then fell into the snow.

Coming into line with SA's moves, Seb joined in her dance, dodging, parrying, and punching his way through the crowd. The cold bit into his exposed skin, but he kept pace with the beautiful assassin and dropped faceless red robe after faceless red robe.

ONCE THEY'D TAKEN DOWN EVERY FOOT SOLDIER, SEB'S world sped up again. He breathed heavily as he surveyed the damage. The reek of cauterised flesh rode the strong winds, lifting the beginnings of a heave in his stomach and forcing him to scrunch his nose up.

Many of the foot soldiers lay dead in the snow. The only ones that hadn't passed were the ones Seb had hit. Before he could think on what he should do with them, Gurt walked through the carnage and executed every one with a shot to the face.

As much as Seb wanted to be brave in front of SA, he flinched to watch a hole bored into the centre of each guard's head. A wet squelch and another acrid kick of seared skin responded to each of Gurt's blasts.

A SEARCH OF THE BODIES ONLY TURNED UP BLASTERS AND one walkie-talkie. Sparks walked out into the bloodstained snow with the walkie-talkie in her hand. She lifted her small computer up next to it and pressed the button to speak into it.

The sound from her computer made no sense to Seb; it

was a foreign dialect he couldn't understand. Because Sparks' computer didn't have a translator chip implanted, it must have been how the soldiers sounded when they spoke to their base.

A few seconds later, Sparks discarded the walkie-talkie and looked at the other three. "I just told them the object on the radar was probably some space junk. That we hadn't seen anything after a thorough search of the mountain."

"So that's why you recorded the other soldiers when they first arrived?"

Sparks smiled, the purple glow of her eyes lighting up.

The snow crunched beneath Gurt's feet as he walked forward and shook his head. "So much for coming in unnoticed. What else has Moses failed to grasp about this mission?"

"I think it's safe to assume our intelligence isn't very," Seb said.

None of the group spoke as the snow swirled around them in the fierce wind.

"Right," Sparks said and clapped her long-fingered hands together. She chewed the inside of her mouth and looked around. "We're on our own from here on out. The first thing we need to do is get away from this place. Someone will come looking for this lot sooner or later."

"Do you think we should hide their bodies in the cave?" Seb said.

"Have you looked around at the snow?" Gurt replied. "Whether we hide them in the cave or not, it's hard to avoid the fact a massacre happened."

Gurt might have had a point, but as always, his words were dripping in condescension.

CHAPTER 23

A dark wood of densely packed trees covered the steep slope down to the edge of the slums of Caloon. Now the group had reached the same level as the slums, they left the fierce cold behind and Seb's numb extremities tingled as they heated up. Or rather, they had not gotten any colder at least. The temperature certainly hadn't reached anywhere close to warm.

At the rear of the group, Seb walked directly behind Gurt. The large Mandulu might have moved with a wide strut, his heavy legs and feet connecting with the ground with a solid *thud,* but he couldn't hide his limp, even if he'd tried. Only subtle—a part of his walk even—Seb had seen Gurt's weakness in the pit simulation, and now it seemed glaringly obvious to him. If the others had noticed, they hadn't said anything yet.

At the front of the line, Sparks flapped soundlessly and jumped to the side of the path as if she'd trodden in something she'd rather not have. She turned and said something to SA and Gurt before Gurt turned to Seb. "Their shit runs through the streets, keep to the side of the path."

A blanket of fog covered the small huts that had seemingly been made from whatever the residents could find. The small dwellings looked to jostle for position in the cramped space. The paths probably only remained free of them because the sewage needed to run somewhere. Despite the waste, at least it gave them a clear route through the place.

Guided by the light of the full moon, Seb looked out over the silver glow of the fog and the thousands of rooftops. Canvas, rusty tin, straw … Like the walls of the small huts, the roofs had been covered over with anything that would do the job.

Despite it being nighttime, many different beings walked the streets. They moved in the shadows with their attention on the ground, and no one spoke to one another. Maybe neighbours communed in the privacy of their homes, but from what Seb had seen so far, it looked like they'd entered a hideously antisocial planet.

The strong ammonia reek of urine and the heady stench of shit forced Seb to pinch his nose as he walked. To breathe through his mouth seemed like the best option. It banished the smell, but he couldn't ignore the fact he had to inhale the noxious atmosphere instead. A slight funk lay as a stale taste on his tongue and he did his best to disregard it.

Although Seb had dumped his ski jacket, he still wore a thick coat. The chill in the air wrapped around his throat, so he zipped up against it. Fortunately both Gurt and SA had also brought coats with them. They might have been carrying enough weapons between them to topple a small planet, but because they hid them, they wouldn't have to deal with the inevitable confrontation the open display of arms would bring.

The fighting pit stood so prominent on the skyline, the party didn't need to talk to one another as they walked toward it. In the wordless streets, they needed to blend in. Behave like the locals and they'd remain invisible in plain sight.

The occasional cry of a small child pierced the air, only to be silenced by their caregiver with cooing and a soft voice. Seb caught smells of spices and cooking meat. Without the spice, it smelled as if the residents were eating tripe; fortunately, he smelled spice more often than not.

AFTER A FIFTEEN-MINUTE WALK, THE GROUP ENTERED A square. Seb looked over at the pit on the skyline. Hard to tell in the foggy dark, but they seemed to have halved the distance between them and it.

The open space—the first one they'd seen since they'd entered the slum—looked like it would be used as a communal area for such things as trading. It currently stood empty, but no doubt saw plenty of activity during the day.

Then Seb heard something and he froze. He looked at the others, and they'd snapped as rigid as him. The heavy thud of boots spoke of an army descending on the square. The dark hid their approach, but as the sound of the marchers got louder, the red cloaks of the Crimson foot soldiers came in from every angle.

Seb's heart jumped into his throat. He drew a deep breath and spoke from the side of his mouth. "I knew we should have hidden those bodies."

CHAPTER 24

The team of four pulled in tight to one another and watched the sea of red descend on them.

"I think we should take the fight to them," Seb said beneath his breath as he watched more cloaks step from the mist and enter the square.

Sparks shook her head. "We're ready for it should we need to be, but let them make the first move; we still don't entirely know where this will end up."

"If we wait, we lose the advantage."

"What if they're not here for us?"

"They're clearly here for us."

The edges of Seb's world had already blurred. He stepped forward and Gurt raised a halting hand at him. "Sparks is right, just wait a second."

"What do you know?"

Before Seb could step forward again, a strong grip wrapped around his left biceps. Ready to throw it off, he turned to meet SA's glowing stare and stopped dead. To have her touch him sent his heart aflutter. A heavy sigh and he nodded at her. She touched him because he needed to chill out, not for any other reason.

Five foot soldiers moved toward them. Tense and ready to go, Seb balled his fists, but the foot soldiers showed no interest in a brawl. Instead, they encouraged the four to step to the edge of the square with a gentle shooing motion of their hands.

"See?" Sparks said as they backed off. "They're not here for us."

The rest of the red robes walked into the square. They came at it from every side as if birthed from the low-lying fog that hung over the place. Once they'd all got in, they formed a ring around the edge. They left just enough space for Seb, his crew, and a few others to stand in the square outside of them. Whatever they had planned at that moment they seemed to have zero awareness of the Shadow Order.

A gap parted in the foot soldiers on the opposite side of the square to Seb and the others. Another two cloaked soldiers walked into the centre with a human boy between them. The kid looked no older than about ten. Skinny, pale, and clearly petrified, he had no defence against the guards on either side of him.

When they thrust him forward, the boy fell and yelped as his skinny knees crashed against the hard and dark stone. He'd landed at the feet of a particularly large soldier. He looked up and the light from the moon caught the glisten of tears against his cheeks. His cherub face hung loose with distress.

The large foot soldier in front of him presented a shiny curved blade to the boy. He offered it as if in reverence of the weapon. It glistened like the kid's tears.

Seb's breath caught in his throat and his stomach turned knots against itself as he watched the boy's fear.

"No," the boy yelled, his voice yet to deepen with the effects of puberty.

The foot soldiers' crimson hoods hid each of their faces in shadow. Despite not being able to see their expressions, their body language—still and unrelenting—said everything it needed to. 'No' didn't exist at that moment. They had expectations the boy needed to fulfill.

The pitch of the boy's voice rose, the confidence of his previous assertion slipping away from him. "Please, I'm not ready for this. I'm only nine. I'm too young."

The lead foot soldier continued to stare down at him. The entire slum seemed to hold its breath as the deep fog swayed and swirled around the place.

The screams of a woman broke the graveyard silence, the sharp sound making Seb jump.

Unlike the boy, who'd been damn near paralysed with fear when he came into the middle of the square, the woman twisted and shook, writhed and kicked.

Nervous adrenaline dried Seb's throat and heightened his nausea. He watched the woman get dragged along by the two foot soldiers. They stood larger than any of the others. The woman's resistance seemed futile against their strength.

As the others had with the boy, the two foot soldiers threw the woman to her knees so she fell before their large leader.

The woman jumped straight back up again, ran to the boy, and enveloped him in a tight hug. Only then did Seb see the familial resemblance. "Damn," he said. The embrace lasted just seconds before the two guards stepped in and ripped them apart.

The curved blade shimmered in the boy's shaking hands. Seb leaned close to Sparks. "What the hell is this?"

Sparks didn't respond.

A pregnant silence damn near choked Seb as he watched the woman in the middle take several steadying breaths before she turned her back to the leader of the foot soldiers, dropped to her knees in front of her boy, and looked up at him. "I love you, Zachary," she said as she cried. "You have no choice but to do this. I want you to remember this *isn't* your fault. You're a slum dweller, and slum dwellers don't get to make decisions. I love you with all of my being, little one."

The edges of Seb's world blurred again. If he needed to, he could break through the line of soldiers in front of him and take down the leader in the middle. But then what? Surrounded by the horrible crimson robes, he and the other three would fall within seconds. They might have been good, but two hundred to four didn't seem like great odds, regardless of their skills.

The boy walked toward his mum with wobbly steps. The blade shone in the darkness. Both the boy and his mum cried freely. The mum looked up at the moon, presenting her neck to her son. "You'll get through the training and become a foot soldier. When you have your turn, remember to keep the compassion that so defines you. Remember *I'm* your mother, not that Crimson bitch in her dark palace."

Gasps ran around the ring from the previously silent foot soldiers and their leader cuffed the woman hard around the back of her head. The wet *snap* of it echoed through the square and knocked the woman over.

She remained on her side on the cold, hard ground and might not have moved were it not for one of the foot soldiers pulling her upright again. The same robed soldier wrapped a grip around her long dark hair and yanked her head back so she stared up at the sky. They'd given her the chance to do it on her own terms only moments earlier, but now they'd taken control.

Seb looked over at SA, who stared back at him, her eyebrows pinched in the middle as she bit down on her bottom lip.

The small amount of light in the sky shone down and showed the movement in the woman's neck from where she gulped. Despite her clear discomfort, she spoke to her boy again. "Do it. You'll overcome this. When you do, be the difference this planet needs. Change this so no one else has to suffer like we have."

Heavy breaths ran through Seb to watch the boy. As someone who'd lost his mum, he wouldn't let himself believe what could happen next.

Barely able to walk with his grief, the boy lifted the curved blade to his mother's neck. His lips buckled out of shape and he mouthed the word *sorry,* his distress choking off his ability to speak.

The boy then yelled as he ripped the knife along his mother's throat.

Seb's stomach lurched to watch a spray of blood cover the boy's front. The kid then dropped the blade and it hit the ground at the same time as his mother did.

The strength drained from Seb's legs to see the boy crumple into a heap, grief robbing him of his strength to stand. A puppet without any strings, the boy sat slumped on the ground, his shoulders shaking as he sobbed.

NOT EVEN A MINUTE HAD PASSED BEFORE ONE OF THE FOOT soldiers entered the square with the rattle of a heavy chain dragging along the ground behind it. Like with all of the others, Seb couldn't determine the gender of the chain carrier as he watched them drag the boy to his feet and clamp a heavy metal collar around his neck.

For the first time since he'd entered the square, the lead foot soldier spoke. His deep voice seemed to come from every angle as if amplified by a PA system. It echoed through the dark walkways of the cramped place. "You have a new family now, boy. The Crimson brotherhood welcomes you into its fold. You'll be a foot soldier like all of us or die trying. We'll look after you better than you could have been cared for down here, and you'll bow down to the mother almighty, the Crimson Countess."

When every foot soldier in the slum repeated, "Crimson Countess," Seb jumped back from the deep stereo sound.

During the ceremonial killing, more foot soldiers had appeared and surrounded the square. The fog hid the potential for even more beyond them. Even if Seb and the others had wanted to leave at that point, they wouldn't be able to. This planet belonged to the Crimson Countess and it shouldn't be forgotten. The residents would come and go when the Countess said they could. A quick glance at each of his friends, and even Gurt looked apprehensive. They had no control here.

CHAPTER 25

It felt like hours had passed, during which time Seb stood with the others as they watched child after child slaughter their family. They didn't try to leave because of the foot soldiers surrounding them. To walk away would be to attract unwanted attention, so they behaved as everyone else did who wasn't in the Countess' employ—they stood by and watched.

Some of the children, broken from the first murder, had to slay mums, dads, brothers, and sisters. One boy had eight family members, and by the time he'd finished, he could barely stand. Even when they clamped the heavy collar around his neck, he fell limp. The children around him remained upright, and Seb looked at his flaccid form, asphyxiating because he couldn't support his own body weight. All the while, the foot soldiers watched on with apparently zero emotion; several of them stared directly at him. Eventually the boy turned limp, throttled by his own body weight.

Sick to his stomach, Seb stood in the metallic funk of spilled blood. The pool in the centre of the square had grown so large, the entire floor glistened. The spilled essence of the families, mixed with the sewage that ran down the hill, flowed through the slum to the forest beyond. 'Let the streets run red' seemed like a phrase reserved for monologues in movies, but now he'd witnessed it with his own eyes …

Utterly helpless, Seb's head spun as he watched every execution. Something compelled the kids to do as they were forced to, and every time another one stepped up, he prayed they would fight it. But they didn't. Each and every one of them—broken to the point of oblivion—killed the people most dear to them. Would he have done the same in their situation? Impossible to comprehend, he thought of his mum and his eyes burned with tears. Bad enough that fate had decided her time was up, what would it have done to him if he'd been the one to end her existence?

When he looked over at Gurt, Sparks, and SA, he saw they'd looked away and he couldn't blame them. But he watched on. If those poor children had to feel it, surrounded by monsters devoid of emotion, then he would feel it with them. If he ever needed a reason to fight on this planet, he'd just witnessed it. Whether they had to rescue some rich imbecile or not, the Crimson Countess' regime needed to be toppled.

By the time the foot soldiers had finished, the line of chained and pale children stretched around the entire square. Fifty to sixty of them. Seb looked at their colourless faces and glazed stares. Whatever the Crimson Countess had planned for them, it had to be stopped.

During the process, Sparks had moved closer to Seb. She now stood so near to him her shoulder rubbed up against his hip. Normally, it would have bothered him and he would have edged away, but truth be told, he needed the touch of a warm body probably as much as she did.

The chain used to shackle the children rattled as one of

the Crimson foot soldiers grabbed it and gave it a sharp tug. The guard then led the children away. As impassive as they'd been the entire time, the foot soldiers in the square watched on as the new slaves trudged toward the elevated city in the middle of Caloon.

ONCE THE SQUARE HAD BEEN EMPTIED OF BOTH BOYS AND soldiers, Seb released a long sigh. For a moment, the group of four stared at one another. He had no words. It seemed like the others didn't either. Their blank stares said enough.

Surrounded by the shadows of the slum and the reek of blood and waste, Seb screwed his nose up. With the foot soldiers gone, vanished into the thick fog, he felt the bite of the cold air again and shivered. He then swallowed against the hard lump of grief wedged in his throat like a golf ball, and said, "Come on, let's make our way to the pit. The sooner we get to the vicious bitch who runs this place, the sooner we can slit her throat."

CHAPTER 26

The group hadn't spoken to one another as they walked in a line through the tight walkways of the slum to the fighting pit. Fog swirled around them and the occasional grunt, roar, or wail shot across the otherwise silent space. Every time Seb thought he'd grown used to the smell of waste, the stench of it seemed to wind up another notch. When they'd entered the slum, the slope had been steep enough that it helped the waste drain away toward the forest on the edge of Caloon. The further in they'd ventured, the flatter the ground. Pools of urine and shit had collected at various points. A foam of stagnation sat on top of them like hardened cream on curdled milk.

Seb had managed to avoid standing in the mess, but with such poor light and an ever-increasing amount of still water, that would undoubtedly change.

As the largest structure in the slum, it remained easy to make their way toward the pit. The closer they got to it, the more beings they saw heading in the same direction. A pilgrimage toward violence. "There must be a fight on," Seb said, his voice croaky for not having spoken for some time.

"Although, it seems odd that they'd fight in the middle of the night."

"Maybe it's the only free time they have," Sparks offered. "With such poverty, I'd imagine it's all about the hustle during the day."

It seemed like a logical explanation.

The four had to slow down when they got to within about fifty metres of the place. The journey toward the pit's entrance had ground to a shuffle. The fighting pit in Caloon seemed as popular as it had on any other planet Seb had been to. Although it had clearly seen better days, it stood as a massive structure to clearly accommodate a huge swathe of spectators who would want to attend. Made from wood, it looked like it had been patched up on more than one occasion. Large panels of differing colours had been nailed to it in random spots like plasters over wounds.

By the time they arrived at the entrance, the press of bodies wedged so close sweat itched beneath Seb's collar. He unzipped his coat to let some of the heat out.

Two Crimson foot soldiers stood on the door. So tall they loomed over most of the clientele. Their hoods hid their faces as they watched the spectators enter.

The button presser in Seb wanted to provoke their silent control, but he kept it to himself. He didn't need to jeopardise the mission because of his ego.

When they entered the packed arena, they had to sit in the back row. The seating ran on such a steep angle it made Seb's head spin. At least it allowed them to see over the people in front of them. He sat down next to SA and nodded at the being on his left. A small creature—about the same size as Sparks—he had white waxy skin that looked like it would peel off him were he to walk in the sun. Very little hair remained on his round head, and he wore a deep scowl when he stared down into the pit as if he needed glasses. Not that they'd be provided on a planet like Solsans.

When the short man looked at Seb, Seb offered him his hand. "Seb."

The creature nodded as he shook it. "Phulp."

"Phillip?"

"No, Phulp."

If Seb said 'Phillip' quickly enough, it would have the same effect.

Silence suddenly engulfed the place and the hairs lifted on the back of Seb's neck. When he caught a whiff of the familiar tang of blood and sweat, he straightened his back and looked down into the pit below. As always, the champion had entered the ring and paraded around it. A brute of a creature, this one had four arms. Although, instead of hands, it had sharp, hardened points that turned each appendage into a spear.

Slow and steady, it walked around the ring and surveyed the crowd.

Unable to contain his giddiness, Seb bounced on his seat. The sides of his world blurred as his gift kicked in. Regardless of the stabby arms, he'd end the creature within one round.

Before Seb could think on it any further, he felt Sparks' attention on him. A look across and he met her purple glare. In the short time they'd spent together, she knew him better than anyone and she knew what went through his mind at that moment. It would be insanity to fight on a covert mission, and he needed that reminder from his small friend.

"I've never been to the pits before," Seb said, testing the water with the creature next to him.

A raised eyebrow met his confession but nothing more.

"How does the betting work?"

"You bet on the champion, Alusta, and collect a small profit when she wins."

"You never bet on the challenger?"

A sharp shake of his head and the man said, "The challenger never wins."

Another encouragement for Seb to go down into the ring, but he held back.

The smallest Crimson foot soldier Seb had seen so far—smaller than Sparks—stepped into the ring and turned to the crowd. "Ladies and Gentlemen, most of you already know her, but please allow me to introduce you to Alusta."

The crowd leapt up. The entire pit shook as they stamped on the ground. Seb grabbed either side of his seat as if that would prevent the place from collapsing. The rickety arena didn't look like it would hold up to much. Unable to do anything about it, he stood up with the others.

Four speared arms raised in the air and the insect-like Alusta spun on the spot to take in the adoration, or frenzy, or bloodlust ... Impossible to tell what the other people wanted when they came to the pit. Personally, Seb liked the sport of it.

A glance to his right again and Seb saw the impassive sheen on SA's face as she surveyed the place. She looked like she knew the position and weaknesses of every creature in the arena. Were it to kick off, she'd fight her way through the crowd and be gone before her victims knew what had hit them. The graceful woman seemed to always have the angles covered.

To let his excitement out allowed Seb to slip deeper into the role of a newbie to the fighting pits. His words came out fast when he spoke to the man on his left. "When does the fight start?"

"Just watch it, yeah?"

Seb wanted to reveal his act. He knew the fighting pits. He knew them as well as anyone—hell, he ruled the places—but he needed to put his ego on the back burner.

A smaller, more lithe creature joined the overgrown insect in the ring and the commentator spoke again as he looked up at the booth occupied by another Crimson foot soldier; this one was clearly a high-ranking representative of the Crimson Countess. "Are you happy with the contender, sir?"

Silence swept through the crowd as everyone turned to the foot soldier in the booth. The large beast paused as he seemed to drink in the atmosphere before he raised a thumb at the commentator. The crowd erupted again.

"Alusta has so far won thirty-nine fights. The record is forty-five and currently held by the purveyor of this fine pit." A pause to look up at the foot soldier in the booth, who nodded for the commentator to continue.

"But can Alusta take it all the way and set a new record? We shall see."

The challenger had a body covered in yellow fur and a wide mouth. With arms and fists like a human, it looked like its killer move rested in its sharp bite. Its jaw had overblown muscles easily as large as Seb's biceps. It looked like it could chomp through steel.

"So without further ado," the commentator called, the touts flying through the crowd as they took the final bets and shouted at the spectators. "Let the fight begin."

The place fell quiet.

CHAPTER 27

The challenger ran at Alusta, dodging and weaving as it charged, its long and lithe body snaking from side to side. To watch—especially at normal speed—showed its strange and hypnotic effect.

Alusta remained perfectly still and waited like a praying mantis, her spear appendages raised.

The challenger screamed and waved its arms.

Alusta stood statuesque, blinking as the yellow furry creature bore down on her.

When the challenger jumped, it led with a punch.

Seb looked at how it opened its powerful jaw. The real attack would come from that. With clenched fists, he imagined himself dodging the blow and driving a hard uppercut to the yellow beast's chin. He'd slam that jaw shut for good.

In a flash, Alusta threw a backhand at her attacker and sent it flying away from her. Her limbs moved so fast, Seb barely saw them. The yellow beast hurtled back the way it had come and crashed into the far wall of the pit.

The crowd gasped to watch the broken form of the challenger slide to the ground. For a second it didn't move, but then it got to its feet, slightly wobblier than before, yet still with the fight in it.

The challenger raised its fists and opened and closed its mouth. Its red forked tongue snapped forward, jabbing the air as if tasting the distance between them. It looked ready to lunge again, but Alusta rushed toward it first. She closed the gap of about ten metres in a flash and appeared in front of her opponent. Two wet squelches and she impaled the slim creature on her spear-like legs.

"Wow," Seb said to Phulp. "Does this kind of stuff always happen in the fighting pits? It's so exciting." Playing the newbie felt like eating glass, but if it helped him ascertain whether he could trust Phulp or not, then it would be worth it.

Phulp didn't respond.

Alusta grimaced as she kept her legs dug into her challenger. The crowd whooped and hollered when she lifted the slim creature from the ground and held it several feet clear of the dusty ring.

The seating area shook from the crowd stamping on the floor and chanting, "End it."

Seb noticed the shake in Alusta's rangy limbs as she continued to hold the challenger aloft. Despite her speed, Alusta didn't necessarily have the strength of some of the other champions. Although, maybe she didn't need it. If he could be an exception for a pit champion, then why couldn't she?

The desire to stand up and challenge her itched beneath Seb's skin, but he remained still. It would serve no purpose. In fact, it would only damage their cause.

With a loud roar that silenced the chaos around them, Alusta pulled her legs apart and ripped her opponent down the middle. Seb jumped and nearly heaved. He hadn't seen that coming! A wet tearing sound accompanied the splash of a body's worth of blood hitting the dusty ground. Like in the square only a short while earlier, the place took on the metallic reek of a slaughtered life.

Two wet thuds echoed as Alusta shook the bisected creature from her arms. Seb watched her take in the audience with a dark glare, her entire form shimmering as if her skin had a mind of its own. If he went down there now, he'd bang her out in the first thirty seconds.

An uncommon action for a pit fighter, Alusta walked over to the large Crimson foot soldier in the booth and dropped down on one knee in front of him.

The shadowed hole where the foot soldier's face should be revealed nothing to Seb. The large brute lifted its hand. A big green fist, skin like leather, appeared from its robe. It raised its thumb at Alusta, the yellowing nail on the end of it long and sharp. Alusta's face lifted with hope and the crowd cheered.

Then the foot soldier flipped his hand and pointed his thumb down.

Silence swept around the pit and Alusta's face fell.

The commentator in the middle of the ring stepped forward and said, "Um … are you sure?"

"Alusta's getting lazy," the large foot soldier explained. "She's not putting on a good show anymore."

Covered in the blood of her opponent, Alusta stared up at the foot soldier but said nothing.

"People come here and spend their hard-earned money gambling on the fights. Alusta's style isn't good for business."

"That's bullshit," Seb said as he leaned close to Phulp. "That was one of the most dramatic fights I've ever seen."

"I thought you said you'd not been to the pits before?"

Seb didn't respond and his face heated up.

After he'd looked at him for a few seconds, Phulp added, "He's the champion and has the record for the most fights. At some point he has to stop Alusta from fighting so he can remain champion. You just saw what she did then. If they let her continue, she won't even have to break a sweat to beat his record."

The two soldiers didn't speak, but the smaller one in the pit continued to look up. Finally, he said again, "Are you sure?"

Utter silence consumed the place before the large soldier's voice boomed around the room. "Finish her."

The Crimson foot soldier in the ring pulled Alusta to her feet, her two more prominent legs still dripping with the blood of her opponent.

Several foot soldiers entered the ring with blasters raised. They all pointed them at the pit's champion, who instead of looking at them, looked up at the large soldier who'd sentenced her to death. As she stared at him, the air lit up with laser fire, tearing through her and dropping her to the ground a second later as a broken and bloody lump.

A glance down the line at his friends and Seb saw all three of them watching the pit, their faces fixed in shock.

The sound from the crowd picked up a second later as they spoke amongst themselves. The foot soldiers dragged Alusta's body away.

Phulp shook his head. "That's such a crappy way to die. The Crimson foot soldiers are power-hungry grunts who like to dominate anyone and everyone. They get humiliated every day by the Countess. By disempowering them, she starts a chain reaction that sees them doing the same to others. The people at the end of the chain take the hardest kick."

Seb needed to hear Phulp's dissent before he trusted him. "Look, I've been to the fighting pits before."

"Obviously."

"But this is my first time on this planet." A quick glance at the other three, who now watched his conversation with Phulp, and Seb said, "The first time for all of us. We're here for reasons I can't go into, but we need to get into the wealthy part of the city."

A shrug and Phulp shook his head. "I'm not sure who can help you do that."

Seb pulled a loaded credit card from his pocket and showed it to the small man. "We can reward whoever takes us where we need to go."

The eyes of an albino—red against his pale skin—widened and Phulp smiled. "Well then, since you say it like that, come with me."

Seb looked at the other three and gave them a thumbs-up.

The five of them stood up and left the pit.

CHAPTER 28

The transition from the fighting pit to the slum brought the acrid reek of waste back to Seb. An involuntary twist gripped his face and he pushed the back of his hand against his nose as he looked at Phulp. "How do you put up with the smell?"

A shrug of his small shoulders and Phulp said, "I've spent enough time here that I don't notice it." He inhaled to the point where his narrow chest puffed out. "It smells like home to me now."

Almost dizzy from the ammonia reek of urine, Seb continued to screw his face up but didn't reply.

The further they traveled from the pit, the narrower the pathways got, so the group fell into single file. They headed deeper into the slum, moving among the foggy streets with the elevated city in front of them. Having left the pits, the cold bite in the air nipped at Seb and he did his coat up to his neck, his shoulders lifting in reaction to the harsh conditions.

The group remained mute as they walked. Many other beings moved through the ramshackle mess around them.

They too kept quiet, their footsteps the only real sound in the place.

Every hut had similar dimensions and were built from junk. The rickety dwellings leaned into one another for support. To pull one down could level the entire slum.

When Phulp stopped, Seb looked around and said, "What are we doing?" His voice carried through the foggy dark and a few beings looked over at him.

Phulp spoke in a whisper. "I need to get something in the shop."

Seb frowned and looked around them. When he glanced at Sparks, SA, and Gurt, they all seemed as confused. "What shop?"

Phulp pointed at the hut directly in front of them that looked the same as all of the others. "I need some food for now and some for later too."

Seb followed Phulp in. Now the canvas door had been pulled aside, he saw the wonky shelves loaded with tins and packs of food. Every product in the place had a long shelf life. Canned, dried, powered ... fresh didn't exist in this shop. And why would it? No shop owner who wanted to survive in such an impoverished place would load their shelves with products that went off quickly. Dust covered some of the tins, while others looked like they'd been recently put on the shelves.

A wrinkly old female stood behind the counter. With a square face like a tortoise and a neck as long, she watched her two customers through large milky eyes. A slight smile rested on her wizened face.

Phulp had a basket on his arm, which he filled with products.

"I thought you said you wanted a *little* bit of food," Seb said.

"And food for later. It's not often I meet someone with your resources. Where the next meal comes from is one of our biggest worries. You can help me alleviate that stress for a while, and I can help you out, yes?"

Hopefully Phulp would be true to his word. Seb nodded at him.

Sparks had come to the door of the shop and she peered into the dark place. A frown crushed her brow as she watched Phulp gather his shopping and then looked at Seb with raised eyebrows. Seb nodded. Were the roles reversed, he would have checked on her too. It felt good to know someone had his back.

THE SHOP DIDN'T PROVIDE BAGS, SO EVERY ONE OF THE group carried several items each as they followed Phulp through the stinking and winding streets again. The small creature weaved through the twists and turns as if driven by an innate guidance system, and as Seb—at the front of his gang—tried to keep up, he also watched the ground for the large pools of urine and faeces.

Phulp stopped outside another hut and Seb rolled his eyes at him. "Another shop?"

The red albino gaze of the waxy-skinned Phulp softened and he smiled. "No. This is my place."

As he entered the small dwelling, Phulp pulled the curtain back and led the group inside.

Built for someone of Phulp's stature, Seb couldn't help but smile at Gurt as he crouched down to get into the place.

"What?" the large Mandulu demanded. His horns pushed up his face as he locked his jaw tight.

Seb laughed. "You look ridiculous crammed into this tiny hut."

Zero humour met Seb's comment.

Each member of the group passed Phulp his food products and he proceeded to stack the shelves in his small dwelling. In one corner he had a fire pit that he must have used for cooking; in the opposite corner he had a pile of blankets and fabrics that he must have slept on. Depression sank through Seb as a heavy weight. "How do you stand to live here?" he asked.

"Huh?" Phulp responded.

"Well, I mean—" Before Seb could say anything else, Sparks silenced him with a sharp elbow in his ribcage.

"What he means," Sparks said, "is that the smell must get to you sometimes. You have a wonderful home, but having to put up with other people's filth right outside your door ..."

A warm smile lit up Phulp's face. "Like I said earlier, I don't notice the smell."

Clearly still riled about the size of the place, Gurt spoke more to himself than anyone. "I don't know how; it bloody stinks."

Ignoring Gurt, Phulp addressed Seb, Sparks, and SA. "If you want to remain off the grid, you stay in the slums. It can be quite beneficial if the soldiers don't know who you are. The surveillance inside the wealthy district is so tight, they know when you've farted and expect you to excuse yourself."

Seb sank a little where he sat. "So you *don't* know how to get us into the wealthy part of the city?"

"I didn't say that. Only that the surveillance is fierce in there. I can get you wherever you need to go on Solsans ... for the right price, of course."

"Well, what are we waiting for?"

"Morning," Phulp replied as he shuffled over to his

makeshift mattress and lay down. "When the morning comes, I'll get you into the heart of the wealthy district. Although, after that, you're on your own. It's not a place I like to stay in for long, and if the Countess finds out I've helped you …" Phulp tailed off and his red eyes lost focus.

Seb looked at the others in his group. SA and Sparks seemed content to rest, while Gurt continued to remain crouched over in the corner, a deep scowl on his angry face.

As much as Seb wanted to provoke him by laughing at him again, he kept his mirth to himself and sat down on the cold and hard ground.

CHAPTER 29

Seb learned of the ambush when he woke up to a loud crash and a sharp pain of something falling down on top of him. Before they'd gone to sleep, Phulp had slipped a wooden pallet across the entrance of his small hut. That pallet currently lay on top of Seb, along with the weight of a Crimson foot soldier pushing down on it.

Everything slowed down as Seb struggled to breathe. Wedged between the pallet and the ground, he shook his head to try to clear the sleep-induced daze from his mind.

Chaos rushed into the small hut as several Crimson foot soldiers entered the place. Two of them pinned Gurt to the ground, and one held Sparks in a headlock. Another one, who acted like the leader of the group, walked up to Phulp.

Smaller than the others, she had a crackle to her voice that dragged sharp fingernails down Seb's spine. Despite being the smallest of the group, she stood in a way that spoke of a confidence in her strength. The little rat held herself like she could bite a windpipe out in an instant.

A quick scan around the small and dark space and Seb

didn't see SA anywhere. He couldn't help but smile to himself.

Two more foot soldiers squeezed in. "How many foot soldiers can you fit in a mini?" Seb said and laughed.

The two newest arrivals stared at Seb, and the one on top of the pallet put more of his weight on it. Pain spread out from Seb's hip as it pressed into the hard ground. They'd obviously come for the four newest arrivals to Solsans and wanted to make a show of it.

The small leader's face remained hidden by the shadow of her hood, but Seb could feel her glare as she stared at him. For a second she remained perfectly still. She then tilted her head to one side. "Who *are* you?"

So maybe they weren't there for Seb and his crew. Seb didn't answer.

The small soldier seemed to lift by an inch as she pulled her chest back and stepped toward Seb. "I said—"

"I heard what you said, and I chose not to answer. So save your breath, yeah?" A quick glance at Sparks and Gurt, and he saw they remained restrained by the guards. SA still hadn't appeared.

"We're here by order of the Crimson Countess and I demand—"

Phulp interrupted her this time. "You're not here on official business. You're here because I owe you money and you've come to collect. Don't pretend it's anything other than that."

Silence filled the small space again and the slight soldier turned back to Phulp.

Still fighting for breath beneath the weight of the heavy soldier and the pallet, Seb shifted to try to find a little more comfort.

A finger click from the lead soldier and the two newest arrivals walked over to Phulp and patted him down.

"So where's my money?" she said, her voice coming out like electrical distortion. The sound scrambled Seb's brain, and were he not incapacitated, then he might have knocked her out just to stop it.

A shake of his head and Phulp stared straight at the soldier. "I don't have it."

The two soldiers who'd searched him pulled away and one of them said, "He hasn't got anything on him." The pair searched the shelves and very quickly found his new stash of food.

After she'd looked at several of the offerings from the soldiers, the leader said, "You seem to have an awful lot of food for a slum dweller."

The slightest shift in the darkest corner of the hut caught Seb's attention. It had to be SA. How they hadn't found her in the small space yet … Before Phulp could reply, Seb said, "I bought it all for him."

The small leader turned to Seb again. "Well, you can pay his debts for him, then."

"No."

"No?"

"You heard me. No. They're not my debts."

Just as the small soldier stepped close to Seb, the bioluminescent glow of SA's eyes opened in the corner of the hut. She crossed the cramped dwelling, and he saw the glint of one of her smaller blades just seconds before she drove it into the throat of the tiny soldier. A gargling noise and the leader fell. Before she'd hit the floor, SA threw a knife at the soldier on top of Seb's pallet, driving him backwards and giving Seb the opportunity to get to his feet.

Seb's world flipped into slow motion again and he saw the beast who'd pinned him grab for the knife in his chest, so he kicked him in the face with a wet *shlop*. It knocked him out cold.

SA took out the two soldiers who'd searched the place. She then went for the ones who had a hold of Gurt, one on each arm. Seb went to Sparks' aid. Before the Crimson guards could react, he'd knocked out his one, and Sparks had killed hers. Several bodies lay on the floor, two of them still fighting against the life leaving them.

Three more soldiers ran into the hut and Gurt shot them one after the other. When the large Mandulu looked at the ones Seb had dealt with, he shook his head. "I'll do your dirty work for you again, then, shall I?"

Although Seb opened his mouth to respond, Gurt had already shot the two soldiers dead.

"We can't leave anyone alive on this mission," Gurt said. "The last thing we need is one of them running to the Crimson Countess to let her know what's coming."

As much as Seb liked to argue with Gurt, he couldn't at that moment. The stocky beast had a good point.

SA stood by the door and peered outside. "Any more?" Seb said.

The brilliant blue glow of her eyes moved from side to side as she shook her head.

In the moments that followed the eradication of the soldiers, the five of them all breathed heavily, but none of them spoke until Phulp finally said, "Oh dear."

They all looked at him, but Sparks replied, "Oh dear?"

"Well, they may not have been here on official business, I do owe them money from a card game, but ..."

"Spit it out," Gurt demanded.

"They were still Crimson foot soldiers. Their deaths won't go unnoticed."

Gurt sniffed and wiped his forearm across his nose before he said, "It ain't the first lot of these cloaked idiots we've killed."

"It's not?"

"No."

"Oh dear," Phulp said again as he gathered up some of his supplies that he'd bought from the shop. "Then we definitely need to get out of here. They'll be looking for you."

IT TOOK NO MORE THAN TEN MINUTES FOR THE FIVE OF THEM to help Phulp pack up his things. "Right," the small and pale creature said, "let's go."

Seb stood to one side to let all the others leave before him. Just before he followed on their heels, he knelt down next to the lead foot soldier and pulled her hood back. The sight hit him like a pit fighter and he nearly fell over backwards. A black and wrinkled face stared back at him. Two deep pits sat where she should have had eyes. She looked like she'd been burned from head to toe, yet she still walked. And she could still see.

"Seb," Sparks called from outside the hut, "we've got to make a move."

Seb shook from the shock of what he'd seen. He remained rooted to the spot for a few more seconds before he got to his feet on wobbly legs and walked out of the place.

CHAPTER 30

Phulp led the way through the dark and tight streets of the slum again. His awkward gait—an almost waddle in the way he tilted from side to side with each step—looked all the more comical for the creature's disproportionately wide shoulders. Seb hadn't seen it before that moment, but the small creature was square. Sparks walked behind him, her rucksack on her back and some of Phulp's food in her hands. They all carried as much of Phulp's goods as they could. After what had happened in his hut, he wouldn't be returning there any time soon.

Gurt strode behind Sparks. Rounded shoulders and a heavy scowl, he kept his blasters hidden but seemed to be itching to draw them at any moment. The graceful SA walked with her chin held high while she scanned their environment. Ever alert, she padded through the dark, windy, and stinking streets like a deity.

Seb—as he had mostly done since they landed on Solsans —took up the rear. The slum seemed to be sleeping because they didn't encounter many beings as they walked along the side of the path, the glisten of sewage in the full moon just inches away from their every step.

"Are you all right, Gurt?" Seb asked the large Mandulu.

Gurt spun around and glared at him. The brute ground his jaw, his horns moving up and down with the mashing movement. After he'd drawn a deep breath, he opened his mouth to speak, but before he could say a word, SA sprang to life. She slipped Phulp's food beneath one arm, shoved Phulp, Sparks, and Gurt into a side alley, and then grabbed Seb before she dragged him into a dark recess on the opposite side to the others.

A shadowy alcove between two huts, they stood so close their bodies touched and Seb could feel the heat that came from her form. The sweet and floral smell he'd yearned for since they were last that close returned. As he listened to her slow breaths—ever calm—he relaxed in her presence.

A few seconds after SA had dragged Seb aside, a loud alarm went off in the slum. The heavy stomp of boots ran toward them down the path. About two dozen Crimson foot soldiers filed past them at a jog. Seb held his breath as he watched them, ready to drop Phulp's food and fight should he need to.

Once they'd passed, SA stepped out into the street and Seb followed. The others came from out of the other side and Gurt looked at SA for a second before he dipped a nod at her. She nodded in return and they set off again after Phulp.

Now the alarm rang through the slum as a whining air-raid siren catcall, it made it harder to hear if someone approached.

≈

SEB REMAINED ON EDGE AS THEY WALKED THROUGH THE streets. Many of the slum dwellers that had come out of their huts since the alarm had sounded watched the group walk past.

Slightly further back than the rest, Seb distanced himself enough so he could avoid the stares from everyone they passed. When they had their attention on the other four, what did one lone traveler matter?

Before they'd gone much farther, Phulp ducked into a hut that looked much like all of the others around them. The rest of the gang followed him in. Seb brought up the rear and chose to sit next to SA as they all made themselves as comfortable as they could be.

"This is my cousin's hut," Phulp said in a whisper once they'd all sat down.

"And he doesn't mind us being here?" Sparks said.

"He's dead, killed by his son in the square."

The statement took Seb back to the images burned into his mind. Throats being cut, blood spraying everywhere, the reek of metal from so much spilled claret. "What was that about?" he asked Phulp.

Phulp's eyebrows pinched in the middle, but he didn't reply. He then drew a deep breath and stammered for a few seconds. The grief of reliving whatever ritual Seb and the others had witnessed seemed to trigger some kind of trauma buried deep within him.

Seb saw Gurt wince at Phulp's discomfort and the large brute spoke. "So why don't we keep going? Isn't it a bit obvious for us to stay in the slum?"

"I'd say the exact opposite, actually," Phulp said, apparent relief on his face at not having to relive his past pain. "As far as the foot soldiers are concerned, I've left my home. They won't assume I have another one. So many people don't even have their own place in here. They won't search the huts; instead, they'll go to the outskirts of the slum."

"You sound like you know the Crimson soldiers pretty well," Sparks said.

Phulp shrugged. "So we're going to be here a while, until morning at least. I don't know about you guys, but I'm not in the mood for sleeping." As he spoke, he opened a can of something, took what looked like a huge date from it, and passed the can around.

When the can got to Seb, he didn't want to seem impolite, so he too took one of the pieces of dried fruit. He hated the taste of dates, but maybe this fruit would surprise him. The sweetness spread through his mouth when he bit into it and he salivated as he chewed. "Wow, what is this?"

"It's one of the only fruits that grows here. It's called a plipple. We export it to the galaxy because as far as I know, no one else has the conditions to farm them."

Seb put the rest of the fruit in his mouth and grinned. "It tastes wonderful."

"I don't want to ask why you guys are here," Phulp said, "that's none of my business, and I'm probably safer not knowing. So tell me a bit about yourselves instead."

Silence swept through the small space until Gurt finally said, "I'm a Mandulu. We're a warrior race that grow up fighting." Gurt pointed to his horns with one of his large fingers. "When we're little, these horns grow all the way up the side of our face. If you fight when you're young, they snap off quite easily during battle. If you wait until you get older, they have to be ground off, which is excruciating. I hated fighting as a kid, but I got used to it."

"Why can't you just leave your tusks to grow?" Seb asked.

"Horns, Seb."

Seb smiled at Gurt.

"Because they eventually grow into our eyes and blind us. They have to be removed one way or another, and it's often done just before we hit puberty. Not only is it more painful to have the elders remove them for you, but it's also more shameful. If you don't lose your tusks in a fight, then you haven't fought enough."

After a deep sigh, Gurt looked at the ground and Seb gasped. "You had to have yours cut off?"

Of all the times Gurt had looked at Seb with malice burning in his red glare, none compared to how he looked at him in that moment. He glared at him with such ferocity now, Seb nearly felt the heat of it. "I *fought*," he said. "I fought a lot. And I won a lot. I was always under the impression that a pretty fighter is the one you should avoid."

"I think so too," Seb agreed. "Someone who's been beaten up a lot suggests someone who can't fight."

"Right? But it isn't like that in my culture. If I've not been beaten up enough, then I'm lazy and I deserve to have my horns ground off. After that day I focused on what I did best." He pulled his jacket open and showed Seb his blasters.

The vulnerability in Gurt at that moment almost warmed Seb to him. Almost.

Although Seb had heard Sparks' story of being orphaned at a young age and living on the streets, when she said, "… and my real name's Louisa Grace," he snorted a laugh.

The others in the hut turned to look at him and Seb's face heated up. "Sorry, I just wasn't expecting that."

Gurt seemed to be reclaiming some of the power he

clearly felt he'd lost when telling them about his childhood. He said, "You thought she was named Sparks from birth?"

"Um, I suppose I didn't think about it." Seb looked at his small friend. "I'm sorry, Louisa Grace."

The tiny Thrystian scowled at him. "I prefer Sparks."

Seb couldn't hide his smile as he dipped a nod at her. "Right-o, LG."

Sparks continued with her story, and once she'd finished, the room turned to Seb. The attention made him uncomfortable and his breathing grew shallow.

"Um ..." he said. "I ... um, I've not got much to say. I was a little shit when I was younger."

"Weren't we all?" Phulp said.

"Yeah, I suppose. I gave my parents hell—not that I cared what my dad thought—but my mum died young and never got to see the man I've become. I used to fight a lot. Unlike Gurt, my culture doesn't like fighting, and those who did it would be outcast and excluded from many situations. I should have paid more attention at school, should have gotten smarter, but instead, I fought people. It was all I wanted to do. It took for my dad to die for me to try to do something else. Although it didn't take long before I ended up in the fighting pits again. I have a brother who also likes to fight like I do. He went too far and killed someone. He's now incarcerated on our planet. He'll never come out again. I think my dad worried I would end up in the same situation, and maybe I would have if I hadn't left the place. Have any of you been to Danu?"

When Seb looked up, the other four all stared at him and shook their heads.

"You don't want to, it's a horrible planet. Dusty all year round. Hot in the winter, burning in the summer. I felt permanently thirsty living there. And the sandstorms ... I'm surprised I have any skin left because of the constant sand-blasting every time I went outside. So, yeah, nothing that exciting, but that's me, really."

The stories of their pasts seemed to lift Phulp, who grinned as he watched the group with his albino stare. "And you?" he asked SA.

Just before Seb could speak on her behalf, she drew a deep breath as if to say something. The hairs lifted on the back of Seb's neck and gooseflesh ran along his arms. The entire planet seemed to stop to listen.

Although quiet, SA sang the most perfect note. Long and drawn out, Seb's mouth hung loose as the gentle tone changed pitch. A celestial lullaby, it came in waves. Seb swallowed back the lump in his throat. When he looked at Sparks, he saw her cheeks dampened with tears and even Gurt seemed to be moved by the song.

The longer SA sang, the more her eyes glowed. The expression seemed to be her truth and Seb squinted in the face of her radiance.

SA finished, blinked away her tears, and dropped her gaze to the ground.

Phulp said it as well as anyone could have. He gasped and uttered just one syllable. "Wow."

CHAPTER 31

Silence filled the hut, and it took Seb a few seconds to notice the chaos had returned outside. When SA sang, everything else had vanished. As he listened to the heavy footsteps of what sounded like more soldiers, he stared at the graceful woman. SA continued to stare at the ground with her eyes closed. When she finally looked up, she locked onto him, the blue glow of her orbs glossy with her tears. Until that moment, he felt like he'd had all the breath dragged from his body by her song. When SA met his gaze, his lungs expelled a little more. She had him in the palm of her hand. He'd never felt so vulnerable.

"This hut isn't comfortable at all," Gurt said, and Seb looked at the brute. Now he'd broken away from SA he suddenly felt self-conscious about the way he'd stared at her, his face on fire.

No one replied to Gurt's comment. Seb shuffled to ease the pain of sitting on the unforgiving ground and he looked at Phulp. Just before he spoke, another stampede of boots rushed past outside. Once it had gone, he said in a whisper, "So what happens now?"

Replying in the same low volume, Phulp said, "We wait until the commotion has died down outside."

Gurt leaned forward with his usual aggression. "Isn't that a bit risky? I'm not sure if you can hear it or not, but it sounds like there's a ton of soldiers outside."

Despite Gurt's confrontational stance, Phulp remained calm. "They won't look for us in the huts. They'll assume we've run away from the slum and go that way. We go outside now and we'll make ourselves much easier to find."

"How do you know that to be the case?" Sparks asked.

"Would you search every hut in this place?" Phulp replied.

Silence, and then Sparks nodded. "Fair point."

"No, the soldiers will probably search for the rest of the night, and they don't know what any of us look like. I'd imagine they'll be bored by morning."

"What about the soldier you owed money to?" Seb said.

Phulp shook his head. "She wouldn't have told anyone other than those with her. Gambling is punishable by death, even for the Crimson foot soldiers."

"So even though some of them are dead," Seb said, "they'll still give up searching for us?"

"The life of a soldier is cheap. They won't waste the resources on the detective work."

Gurt leaned from the shadows again and stared down at Phulp. "You seem to know a lot about the soldiers."

Silence returned to the hut. The alarm continued to pulse outside and footsteps ran back and forth, but at that moment, Seb and his three team members all stared at Phulp.

Their small and pale host looked like he knew he had to answer carefully. "I … uh, used to be one of them."

Seb blinked and Gurt had already drawn his gun and aimed it at Phulp.

"Pretty much every adult male in this place used to be one of them."

Gurt kept his gun raised. "And you aren't one now?"

"Do I look like one?"

Instead of replying, Gurt kept his gun up.

"*No*," Phulp said. "I'm not a soldier anymore. I told you this hut used to belong to my cousin before his son killed him, right?"

None of the others spoke.

"Well, the Crimson Countess has a special recruitment process for her foot soldiers." A distant look washed over Phulp's red eyes. "From time to time, she takes as many teenage boys as she can find and rounds them up. She then forces them to kill all their loved ones before she puts them in the training camps."

"We saw that in the square," Seb said.

"With no family left," Phulp continued, "you exist in the pens and call her mother. They take years to make sure the soldiers are totally subservient to the Crimson Countess—or at least for them to believe they are subservient to her. If you can't convince the regime that you're loyal, they throw your body over the ledge of the city down into the slums below. The truth is, it seems that most of the soldiers hate the Crimson Countess."

"Why don't they overthrow her, then?" Sparks asked.

"Fear. You've seen the size of her army. That's a lot of people to persuade she needs to be overthrown. We don't talk to one another with any kind of depth. You say the wrong thing to the wrong soldier and you end up dead. So even if I did find like-minded soldiers, the risk of finding one who would sell us out seemed too great. Living in Caloon is a daily reminder that you don't own your life, she does. It's a simple fact that those who march to the beat of her drum live longer."

Seb replayed the massacre in the square. "So you had to kill …"

"My mum, dad, and baby sister." After a heavy sigh, Phulp said, "She was only two. When she saw me kill Mum and Dad, she cried louder than I'd ever heard her cry before. I thought she'd be too young to understand, but she ran straight to me for comfort." Phulp sighed and ran a shaking hand over his pale head. "I held her with the blood of our parents on my hands. The foot soldiers then gave me a knife and pulled her head back to expose her throat."

SA gasped and Seb looked at her, his stomach turning in against itself.

"So when you were one of the soldiers, you had to do the same to young boys?" Seb asked.

Another heavy sigh and Phulp looked at the ground.

Before he could reply, Seb said, "It's okay. I don't need you to answer that."

"So," Phulp said, "although I hate the Crimson Countess, and whatever you're on this planet to do is fine by me, just know how much of a risk I'm taking to try to get you into the city."

"You're not doing it for free." After Seb had said it, he felt like a complete dick.

"No, you're right, and I wouldn't do it for free, but the fact that I'm putting my life at risk doesn't go away, regardless of how much you pay me."

Shame made Seb slump where he sat and he felt the others look at him. "I'm sorry. I can see that. Sorry."

Phulp shuffled as if to make himself comfortable on the hard ground. "That's okay," he said as he curled up into a ball like a domestic cat. "Let's get some rest. We're going to need it for the morning."

Why did Seb have to be such an arsehole? Although he thought about speaking again, he had nothing that could undo what he'd already said. Instead, he copied the others in lying down. Despite his extreme discomfort, exhaustion won out. When Seb closed his eyes, he instantly fell asleep.

CHAPTER 32

E verything ached when Seb woke up. Sore from the cold, hard ground, he groaned as he stretched the tiredness from his body. Upon properly opening his eyes, he saw everyone else had already woken up and they all stared at him.

"Um … uh, how long have you guys been up for?"

"A while," Gurt said. "I said we should have woken you. I was up for dropping a bucket of water on your head—" he flashed Seb a facetious smile "—bucket and all."

Seb forced the same facetiousness back through his tired haze. Like in the last hut, the entrance had been blocked by scrap wood to act as a door, although it didn't quite fit as tightly as the other one had. A look outside showed him it remained dark. He relaxed again. "Will someone wake me up when it's morning?"

"It is morning," Phulp said.

Seb sat up again. "Huh?"

"It's morning."

When no further explanation came, Seb looked at Sparks, who said, "It's always dark on Solsans."

"Always?"

She rolled her purple eyes. "Always."

"My god. How long before we get off this cursed planet?"

Gurt spoke this time. "Well, if you didn't spend the entire time asleep, then we would be going a lot sooner."

"You should have woken me up."

"I *know!*" Gurt said. "But, like I said, the others wouldn't let me."

"Well, moan at them." With his glare fixed on Gurt, Seb added, "They might actually care what you have to say."

A scowl crushed Gurt's fat face, but before Seb could say anything else, a shrill whistling sound flew through the air. A second later white light flashed through his vision, temporarily blinding him. The ground shook like an earthquake ran through it, and the sound of tearing wood accompanied the hut collapsing around them. A thick cloud of dust kicked up from the fallen wood, which blinded him further as his world flipped into slow motion.

Seb's head spun and his ears rang. He rubbed his stinging eyes. The brick dust itched his throat and he wheezed when he breathed. Thick smoke made it almost impossible to see, but he could just about make out the large form of Gurt in the hut with him. It looked like everyone else had gone.

The smoke and dust continued to blind Seb, but with a fierce heat coming from one side of them, both he and Gurt moved against the far wall of the hut. It felt like the only strong wall of the structure, the one wall that kept the shack standing.

As the dust settled, Seb saw the orange glow of flames streak through the black smoke. A large beam had fallen across their path and burned bright. It blocked their exit. He turned to Gurt, but before he could speak, Gurt drove a hard punch into the solid wall they leaned against. It made a loud *thwack,* but the wall didn't budge.

The weak spots of his surroundings came to Seb. Gurt's chin, his damaged right knee, the beam. But no matter what part of the solid wall he looked at, he couldn't see any frailty to it.

In his panic, Seb's heart sped up and he breathed quicker, pulling in more of the dark black smoke that filled their cramped space. His eyes stung and tears streamed down his cheeks. The thick and dark clouds stuck to his skin like tar.

Another punch against the wall and another loud *thwack* before Gurt shoved Seb. "Do something. Help me try to get us out of here."

"The wall won't break."

Gurt gave it another whack, so hard it shook the ground. "How do you know?"

"Trust me."

Thwack.

Thwack.

Thwack.

Repeated hits did nothing. In Seb's slowed-down state, he saw Gurt's large fist bleed when he hit the wall again.

The smoke initially rose and filled the roof space of the hut, but it now pushed down on top of Seb and Gurt. Seb lay on his front to get as far away from it as possible.

Gurt followed his lead and the two of them lay nose to nose.

"How are we going to get out of here?" Gurt asked, his red eyes wide.

Seb shook his head. His lungs tightened with every inhale, his head spun, and the plastic taste of burned rubber stuck to the back of his throat. "I'm not sure we can."

CHAPTER 33

The smoke rose to give Seb a clearer view when he pressed his cheek against the cold ground and looked along it. The gap under the flaming beam seemed tiny. No way could he or Gurt sneak beneath it. He drew shallow breaths into his tight lungs to try to combat his panic. The urge to cough burned in his dry throat and made his eyes water worse than ever. The coughing itself would be fine. However, the deep inhale after each one would drag the poisonous air into his lungs and turn his lights out.

A shadow moved across the gap outside and Seb suddenly saw one purple eye staring back at him. He spoke with a wheeze and so quietly that she wouldn't be able to hear him. "Sparks?"

The bespectacled eye blinked several times. If she did try to talk to him, Seb heard nothing over the roar, pop, and crackle of the fire.

Another explosion shook the ground and Seb heard screams come from a way off. Some more dust fell from the ceiling above him. Tears blurred his eyes, and although he couldn't see clearly, he recognised the bottom of Sparks' rucksack when she put it down on the ground outside.

A second later Sparks slid something metal into the small gap beneath the flaming beam. It looked like a miniature car jack. When she wound a handle, it grew taller and lifted the beam with it.

Seb watched Sparks' large hand spin the handle until it locked at full height. Still too tight for him to get out, and certainly too tight for Gurt, Seb wanted to call out to Sparks to ask her what she planned to do. But the more breath he used, the closer he would get to passing out.

Then Seb saw Sparks' face again. Her purple eyes spread so wide it looked like her eyeballs would fall out. She ducked down low and crawled beneath the flaming beam, every pop and crackle making her jump as she moved.

Once inside, Sparks reached back through the gap for her bag and dragged it under. On its way through, it caught the jack, pulled the bottom away from it, and the device collapsed, the beam coming down with it. It landed flush with the ground and left no space to reinsert the jack.

By the time Sparks had crossed the small hut to Seb, her eyes streamed with tears. Her hands shook as she rummaged around in her bag. When she'd retrieved a small metal device, she handed it to him and shouted over the roaring fire. "Stick this to the ceiling and press the red button."

Seb had no time to question her order, so he drew a deep breath, stood up in the smoke, and did exactly as Sparks had said. When he dropped back down again, he saw Sparks had unfolded a large fireproof blanket, which she pulled over the three of them.

Sparks counted down from three. On one, Seb heard a pop and then a fizz before Sparks said, "We can look again now."

Although still smokey, the entire room had been covered in white foam that had put the fire out. Sparks threw the blanket away from them, pulled a small blowtorch-like device from her bag and cut into the wall that Gurt couldn't break through.

It only took a few minutes, during which time Sparks needed to pull back down several times to ground level so she could breathe away from the smoke, which, although thinning considerably, still hung heavily enough to choke them. She finally managed to cut through to the neighbouring hut.

Gurt hit the wall this time and it crumbled, allowing the three of them to get through.

Once they all got outside, Seb let his cough go. Deep seal-like barks bucked through him as the cough gathered momentum. Stars swam in his vision from the effort and he heaved several times.

When Seb felt a hand on his back, he turned to see SA smiling down at him. A second later, a hot rush of vomit leapt into his throat and he didn't have time to turn away before he threw up all over SA's shoes. Barely able to see for his tears and with the taste of sick seared into the back of his nose, he put a hand across his mouth. "I'm so, so sorry."

SA smiled as she continued to rub his back.

ONCE HE'D RECOVERED, SEB WALKED OVER TO SPARKS AND gripped her in a tight hug. She made fake gargling noises at his affection and he whispered in her ear, "Thank you. Thank you so much. I know how much of a big deal that was. Thank you."

Sparks flushed red as she pulled away from Seb, and

before she could respond, a high-pitched *whoosh* tore through the air above them.

Seb looked up to see a ship race through the dark sky. A second later it dropped another bomb. Far enough away not to cause any immediate danger to them, he watched the plump device fall into the slum. The explosion shook the ground and a huge mushroom cloud of grey smoke rose into the sky. Wind rushed out from the blast and blew his hair back from his forehead. "What the …?"

Phulp had stood by them for the entire time, but it took for him to speak for Seb to remember he was there. "This happens sometimes. We get attacked from neighbouring planets because they want to take our resources. The Crimson fleet should be here soon."

Although still blurred, Seb's sight had improved since he'd stepped out of the burning building. He saw the black ships with red stripes along them. They tore through the air after the bombers, their laser fire going painfully wide.

"They're nearly as accurate as you, Seb," Gurt said. "No wonder they bomb this place, it's not like there's much of a deterrent not to. Give me a catapult and I'll probably be more of a danger to the enemy ships than those clowns are."

As Seb watched the bomber fly away, he shook his head. Gurt normally talked utter nonsense, but he had a point; the Crimson fleet couldn't shoot at all. Of all the foot soldiers they could use, why pick the ones with such terrible aim?

The devastation on the ground took Seb's attention away from the sky. Half of the slum remained on fire and dark smoke turned the black sky even blacker. Coughs and splutters surrounded him. Creatures wailed, brayed, and cried while the pop and crackle of fire ran as a constant background noise. It would take some time for the vast blaze to burn out.

The huts being so close to one another would give the flames free rein to travel across the slum.

CHAPTER 34

If the streets through the slums had seemed narrow before, they now felt claustrophobic. Seb sweated from both their quick pace and the heat around them as he walked at the front of the pack directly behind Phulp. The slum burned on either side of them and the flames reached up into the sky. They touched at points above their heads, forming an archway of fire over them.

Like when he'd been in the hut, the smoke in the streets stung Seb's eyes. Thick, acrid, and blinding at times, it rode the wind, choking him whenever a dense enough cloud hit him.

The smoke clung to Seb's skin like soot and felt gritty every time he wiped the waterfall of sweat from his face.

Seb swallowed several times, but it did nothing to rid the taste of molten plastic from the back of his throat.

The screams and cries of what sounded like the suffering of a thousand different creatures surrounded the gang. But they could do nothing to help. Instead, they walked with their heads down, pushing deeper into hell with every step forward.

When Seb glanced behind, he saw Sparks close to him, muttering something to herself as if she needed the constant reassurance to keep going.

Phulp, who seemed totally at ease with the situation, looked back at Sparks and then smiled at Seb. "You have a good friend there, you know? You can see how fire makes her feel. Scared is normal, but for her, it goes beyond that."

Another glance at the small Thrystian and Seb nodded. "We weren't always friends, but I'm glad we are now. You're right, she'd follow me into hell and back, and I her." He looked beyond Sparks and saw SA walking with her usual grace, seemingly impervious to the scorching chaos around them, and Gurt moving along with his slight limp disguised by his alpha male gait.

"This is the best time to travel, you know," Phulp said, pulling Seb's attention back to him.

"Why's that?"

"The Crimson foot soldiers tend to keep a low profile when the slums burn."

"That makes sense." Seb then said, "This happens often, does it?"

"Yeah." Phulp looked around. "Whatever resources we have on this planet, it seems a lot of people want them. The Crimson star fleet are always fighting in the skies."

"Is that what you call it?"

"Huh?" Phulp said.

Seb shook his head. "Don't worry." The Crimson star fleet and their inability to shoot didn't matter. He thought of the slightly pudgy, floppy-haired Camoron instead and drew as deep a breath as he could without choking. They wouldn't be here were it not for his greed.

Before Seb could think on it any further, a large female— taller than him, red-skinned, and with three horns down the centre of her face—ran from the flames. Her eyes were spread wide and she had the blackened body of a little one in her arms. It bore the same horn formation as her.

It took just one glance at the charred and smoking body to see the child had died, but she didn't seem ready to accept that yet. Phulp grabbed Seb's arm and pulled him aside to let her through. The others in their party did the same as they watched the creature run down the pathway with her dead child, her bare feet splashing in the sewage.

Bile burned the back of Seb's throat. "Such devastation. You'd think with the number of foot soldiers the Crimson Countess has, she'd take the fight to these planets rather than letting them come in and create chaos like they do."

"The city is much more fiercely protected than the slums," Phulp said.

"So it's no great loss to her?"

"Apparently not."

"Do they ever manage to bomb the elevated city?" Seb asked.

"Not that I've ever witnessed."

Surrounded by the popping and crackling sounds of buildings on fire, Seb heard a different noise. A tearing, crashing sound. He heard creaks and groans followed by loud slams. A look to his right and he saw a group of giant creatures working through the slum, knocking down huts.

When they came across one, a large brute of a monster stepped out before they could level it. Purple and marked with black tribal tattoos all over its body, it had a chest so broad Seb wondered how it managed to stay upright. When it roared at the group of demolition experts, Seb felt the reverberation of its fierce warning against his chest.

Before Seb could ask Phulp about the destruction of the

huts, the small and pale creature rushed off to help the demolition crew.

Despite being mobbed by five creatures, the purple beast
still put up a good fight.

Seb ran through the huts to join Phulp. SA and Gurt had
joined him too. Sparks remained on the path, and Seb
couldn't blame her. She'd gone above and beyond already
today.

Seb, Gurt, and SA joined in and they managed to wrestle
the big monster to the ground. It bucked and writhed, and
when it roared again, the volume of it blurred Seb's vision.
"You can't destroy my home."

One of the demolition crew shouted back as he rode the
bucking brute, the chaos of their surroundings forcing
urgency from everyone as the temperature rose from the fire
creeping closer. "If we don't make a gap in the huts, this fire
will burn through the entire slum. Your hut won't make it
either way. Better to knock it down and save everyone
else's."

The large beast growled as it fought to pull breaths into its
wide chest. The inhale and exhale of the monster lifted Seb
and the nine others who lay on top of it.

Once they'd pulled its hut down, they got off him. The
destruction of its home had robbed the purple creature of its
fight and it slumped in defeat. Phulp led the way back to the
path. The other three followed and they joined up with Sparks
again.

They continued their journey toward the elevated city, and
Seb asked Phulp, "Does that work? Pulling the huts down?"

A shrug and Phulp nodded. "Yeah. Usually."

The closer they got to their destination, the less the fires
burned.

Hardly surprising considering what Phulp had said about the elevated part of Caloon avoiding attacks.

The dark sky had cleared enough for Seb to search it for signs of more ships, but he thankfully couldn't see any.

Such poor visibility meant Seb didn't realise just how close they'd got to the elevated part of the city until they were virtually on top of it. To look up at it made him dizzy. If there were any clouds on Solsans, the city would have nestled among them for sure. But since he'd been there, the sky had remained clear.

From a distance, it seemed like the elevation had been natural. But now Seb was closer, he could see the work that had gone into it. Stones stacked one on top of the other and held in place with cement showed the huge and wide protrusion had been elevated with intent.

PHULP TURNED TO SEB AND SAID, "CAN I TAKE MORE OF MY credits as payment, please? You don't have to give it all to me, but I'm taking a huge risk here, and I want to make sure I get paid something at least."

After a glance at the others, Seb received their nods of approval before he took the empty card Phulp held out to him and transferred over a large proportion of the credits he'd promised him.

Phulp then grabbed Seb's arm and yanked it. A loud *slam* landed behind him. Seb turned around to see the broken body of a boy where he'd stood moments earlier. The kid had a waxy look to him that was similar to Phulp. He must have been about fifteen and lay with his mouth open wide, his black eyes glaring from his dead face.

Instant dryness spread through Seb's throat as he looked down at the boy. "What the …?"

"A failed Crimson foot soldier," Phulp said while he stared at him, zero emotion on his blank face. "It's what I told you about earlier. If they don't make the grade or they fail to show convincing devotion, the Countess throws them out of the city … literally."

When Seb glanced at the rest of his crew, he saw they all watched him with the same shocked expression.

"Come on," Phulp said as he stepped through an archway built into the bottom of the city. "To get into the elevated part unnoticed, you have to go through the sewers."

The reek of the smoke had been in Seb's nostrils until that point. When he stepped forward, he caught a stench worse than any he'd smelled since arriving on Solsans. The streets running through the slums stank, but now they'd come to the source of the sewage, it made his eyes water. "No wonder you can get through here unnoticed." He pressed the back of his hand against his nose to mask the smell. "Who in their right mind would search this place?"

Darker than any part of the city, the stench of waste hung so thick in the air, Seb could taste it as a stale funk on his tongue. The obsidian walls glistened, damp as if sweating the ammonia reek of the place. Like in the sewers below Aloo, they had thin walkways running next to the vile rivers.

Once they'd traveled about fifty metres into the place, a light flicked on and Seb turned around to see Sparks with her mini-computer in her hand. He nodded and then smiled at her.

"So do all of the Crimson foot soldiers end up living in the slums once they've done their service?" Seb asked Phulp.

"The lucky ones do."

"The lucky ones?"

"Yeah. Sometimes the Countess takes a shine to you. You don't want that to happen because she'll employ you as one of her personal guards. There isn't any getting away from that. Fortunately, because of my size, she barely noticed me." Phulp stopped dead.

When the others stopped too, Seb heard it: the scratch of feet walking across stone.

Despite speaking in a whisper, Phulp's voice carried in the enclosed space. "There's someone down here with us."

CHAPTER 35

The group remained both silent and still as they listened to the being approach them. The dry rasp of a foot dragging along stone called at them from the darkness. A slap of a heavy step hitting the ground followed by the dry rasp again.

The hairs on the back of Seb's neck stood on end and his heart beat faster. Swallowing both the musty taste of the stinking sewers and a mouthful of sticky saliva, he stood tense and waited.

Each step forward brought the being closer to appearing from the shadows. But, as yet, it remained hidden.

A shrill cackle then came from the darkness. It rang out, stuttered and flighty as if the person laughing had zero control over the sound. The sharp mirthful noise echoed through the caves and ran away from them down the many tunnels.

Seb heard the water break next to him as if something had pushed up through the surface, but when he looked down, he saw nothing in the excrement-filled sludge.

The laugh came again. An erratic titillating noise, it

turned Seb's blood cold. At the sound of movement behind him, he spun around to see Gurt and SA step up to his flanks. Both of them had their weapons drawn and both of them stared into the darkness as if ready to attack.

The sides of Seb's world blurred, and he too fell into a slightly more defensive crouch. If it kicked off, they'd be ready.

Another splash sounded out down to Seb's left and he looked at the water again. Because Sparks stood at the back of the group, her torch didn't provide the best light and he couldn't see what moved in the dirty liquid next to them.

Seb instantly forgot about it when a human emerged from the darkness. So pale she almost glowed, her hair hung from her red, raw scalp in chunks. It looked like large handfuls of the dark locks had been pulled out. Probably by her.

She dragged one lifeless foot behind her as she walked, and she continued to giggle while getting closer to the group.

Seb caught Gurt in his peripheral vision raising his gun, so he pressed on top of the barrel and encouraged the Mandulu to lower it. "She looks crazy," Seb said, "but she doesn't look dangerous."

"You wouldn't give her a chance if she wasn't human."

And maybe Gurt had a point. Maybe coming from the same gene pool as the deranged figure in front of them did make Seb more empathetic.

Before Seb could answer Gurt's accusation, Phulp said, "Sewer dweller."

The woman continued forward, completely oblivious to Phulp's assessment of her.

"They can't survive in the slums, so they come to the sewers and sift through the waste of the wealthy."

"There's something worth scavenging down here, is there?" Gurt asked.

"If not, they've been known to resort to eating …"

Before Phulp could finish, the woman got closer and Spark's torchlight flashed across her face. She had no teeth and her jowls were coated in what looked like dry shit. Seb stepped back a pace.

The woman locked a glassy stare on Seb as she closed in on him. A zombie with an insatiable hunger, she seemed to only care about him at that moment. She giggled again as if the excitement of being in his presence overwhelmed her.

"Looks like you've got a fan," Gurt said.

The woman raised her right arm and pointed a shaking finger at Seb. The water broke next to them again and he glanced down. Something moved in it.

"It's you," the woman said, her voice scratchy.

Seb stepped back and said, "Huh?"

"The one! It's you. I thought it was you, but I had to be sure."

"What are you talking about?" The water broke again, and Seb looked down quickly enough to see a thick tentacle covered in suckers. As much as he wanted to turn to the others, he couldn't take his eyes off the crazy woman who'd gotten to within a few metres of him. When he saw that she had all of her teeth, he heaved. She'd appeared toothless because of the amount of shit in her mouth.

She worked her jaw as she chewed on the brown substance and she giggled some more. "Our saviour," she said, the reek of waste riding her words. "The son of the special one. You have the gift."

The woman reached forward to touch Seb and he recoiled, heaving at her stench. She hissed at him and snarled. "Let me touch you. I've waited my life in these sewers because I knew you would come. Let me—"

Before she could say anything else, a loud splash sounded

out next to them and a huge tentacle burst from the water. As thick as Gurt's thigh, it had suckers along the bottom of it. A lasso, it wrapped around the woman's ankle and ripped her from her feet.

The woman's scream disturbed Seb more than her laugh. Pure high-pitched fear, it hurt his ears and he winced to watch her hit the hard ground with a thud and then get dragged toward the water.

"We need to run," Phulp said. "Now!"

Although Seb heard Phulp's words, he couldn't move as he stared at the spot the woman had occupied just seconds ago. The river ran as if nothing had happened. The woman and the tentacle had vanished beneath its surface.

Phulp, Sparks, and SA all sprinted past Seb, yet he still didn't move. It took for Gurt to grab Seb's arm and drag him with them before Seb followed the group into the darkness and away from whatever had just pulled the woman under.

CHAPTER 36

Phulp took off at a sprint, opening a gap between him and the others. He ran so fast he even left Sparks behind.

Seb shook his head. How did creatures so much shorter than him manage to outpace him?

With his lungs still aching from the fire in the hut, Seb sped along the damp and narrow footpath. It looked like it should be slippery, but didn't feel it … yet.

It seemed that Sparks did her best to hold her torch up, the white light wobbling as she ran with it. However, it did little to illuminate the dark tunnels. They'd have to follow their guide. Phulp's pale skin helped keep him visible and made the short squat creature almost glow in the dark.

Although, when the others—led by Phulp—rounded a sharp turn, Seb completely missed it. As his world slipped into slow motion, he felt his leading foot slip as he tried to step on a piece of the path that didn't exist. Sparks must have turned his way because her torch lit up the frothy water below, showing him the brown stools floating in it. Some were as long as his leg.

Just before Seb took the plunge, Sparks grabbed his shirt. Not only Sparks, but SA and Gurt held on too, anchoring the small Thrystian woman, therefore anchoring him and pulling him back to safety.

Out of breath and without time to thank them, Seb watched Sparks and the others take off after Phulp again, and he followed directly behind them.

The large river of waste narrowed around the next bend and they saw Phulp as he hopped across to the other side. They all followed him a few seconds later.

The place still stank; Seb only smelled it when he thought about it, but he'd already started to get used to the reek, which somehow disturbed him more than the stench itself.

Several more turns and Seb called ahead for the others to wait, his loud voice echoing through the dark and dank tunnels.

Phulp pulled up, as did Sparks and the others.

"Surely we've lost it now?" Seb said. He looked down at the water. "I haven't seen anything move down there since we started running."

The silhouette of Phulp moved in some way, but it took for him to step into Sparks' torch beam for Seb to see him shaking his head. He looked as exhausted as Seb felt, his small chest rising and falling as he gasped for breath. "No," he finally managed. "It may look …"

Before he could say anything else, the sound of rushing water preceded a huge tentacle rising from the funky river.

It wrapped around Gurt like a constrictor, and although Seb worried for Gurt's safety, he couldn't help but cringe at the slimy appearance of the beast.

Solid in his stance, Gurt held his position long enough for SA to pull out one of her larger knives and stab the tentacle.

The beast let go with a scream that shook the walls around them, and it instantly withdrew, the tentacle rushing back to the water so fast it turned into a blur.

Phulp didn't need to say anything else. When he took off again, they all followed.

CHAPTER 37

After every laboured breath—his smoke-damaged lungs tight—Seb wanted to call out for the group to stop. The labyrinthine tunnels and rivers seemed to never end and he didn't have it in him to run forever.

When they came to an open space, Phulp halted. They'd arrived at a square room where the rivers crossed in the middle. A large piece of damp path sat in each corner. "This … seems … like the … best … place to stop and … fight it," he said between breaths. "We won't outrun it."

Seb looked at the others and they all nodded at one another. They took a corner each and Phulp retreated into a dark tunnel.

Seconds later, the rush of water raced into the room, and for a moment everything stilled.

Then—as before—a gushing noise like a large waterfall sounded out as something rose in the middle of them. Somewhere between a squid and an octopus, the monster had thick green skin and a domed head.

Two eyes, each as large as a dinner plate and black like the darkest corner of space, stared at Seb before it stretched open two vast wings. The span—about five metres wide—spread across the entire space. The beast spun on the spot to take in its opponents. Flaps of shredded skin hung down over its mouth like torn fabric. Fleshy and loose, they swayed with the creature's movement.

Everything had slowed down for Seb and he noticed Sparks in his peripheral vision as she slipped a watch onto her wrist.

The beast locked onto Seb again and opened its wide mouth. Big enough to swallow him whole, the stench of rot and decomposition rode on its breath. When it inhaled, the rush of wind pulled him forward a step before it screamed. The shrill call pierced his eardrums and blew him backwards. The creature shook with the force of its call, the loose flesh in front of its mouth blowing outwards from the release.

Something about the sound rattled Seb's entire being. It jangled his nerves and implanted the memories of nightmares into his psyche. If he walked away from there today, he'd be taking that sound with him. Like an owl shocks its prey with its screech, he became momentarily paralysed by the aggressive yell of the beast.

Even though Seb looked at it through a slowed-down world, the beast moved as quick as a flash, slamming one of its tentacles next to Sparks. The force with which it hit the ground sent a shockwave rushing away from the impact and shook dust from the ceiling above them.

Sparks dodged out of the way in time and pressed her watch. A bright magnesium glare sprang from her wrist and earthed on the wet tentacle of the beast. Like it did when SA stabbed it, the monster withdrew.

Another loud scream and the creature lifted a tentacle above Gurt. Before it brought it down, Gurt sent several blaster shots into it, again, scaring the beast away. Regardless of its retreat, the shots seemed to have little impact against the large monster's thick hide.

When Seb saw a tentacle rise in front of him, he felt a spray of sewage come with it. Only a small amount, it still splattered against the skin on his face and he winced at the sensation.

The tentacle crashed down, but Seb's current state allowed him to see it and dodge to the side.

The beast raised its tentacle again and slammed it down a second time, each slam against the ground a heavy thud like the others had been.

Seb dodged it again and noticed SA sprinting in his direction.

As Seb avoided a third blow from the dark green tentacle, SA leapt across to his square of path. She faced the beast while flying through the air and threw two knives at it. Both of them glinted in what little light they had down in the tunnels, and each one scored a direct hit in each of the beast's eyes.

The monster screamed so loud it shook the walls. Blinded by SA, it pulled back into the river, disappearing beneath the surface.

Before it got away from them, Sparks ran to the edge of her path and used her watch to fire another magnesium bolt of electricity into the water. The entire tunnel lit up blue and buzzed.

All four of the team gasped for breath as they stared down at the river. A splash, much quieter than before, and the body of the beast floated to the surface. If Sparks hadn't killed it, she'd certainly knocked it out.

Phulp emerged from his dark bolt-hole, a smile on his squat face. "Well done, guys. I've never seen one killed before." For the next few seconds, he stared down at the beast and shook his head. "Amazing." With a clap of his hands, he looked back at the four. "And now we need to get out of here. I hate to think what will happen if its mother comes after us."

"Mother?" Gurt said.

"Yeah, that one was only a baby."

CHAPTER 38

The group walked at a much slower pace with Phulp infinitely more relaxed in the lead. They made sure to move with as much stealth as they could manage in the dark. If Phulp had spoken the truth about the monster being a baby, they'd have to keep the noise down and pray they didn't run into the mother.

Seb walked with SA behind him and Gurt in front. While speaking in a whisper, he turned to SA and said, "Great shot with the monster's eyes, by the way."

The assassin's stare lit up as it always did and she dipped a very slight nod of gratitude.

When Seb saw Gurt turn around with a sneer on his face, he cut him off before he could pass comment. "You look like you're walking a bit more easily now."

Gurt stopped and scowled at Seb. "Huh?"

"Earlier, you looked like you had a slight limp, like, I dunno, you'd hurt your right knee maybe."

It only flashed across Gurt's eyes for the briefest of moments, but vulnerability crossed the large brute's features nonetheless. After the moment had passed, Gurt growled at Seb. "What are you talking about, fool?"

Seb stared into the red glare of the Mandulu and flashed him a facetious smile. "I'm not sure, maybe I'm talking nonsense."

"I'd say so."

Before Seb could respond, Gurt had turned his back on him and walked off.

The wash of water bubbled along beside them and drips called through the cavernous tunnels. Sparks' torch did a good job of lighting the way, but it brought the shadows around them to life. The darkness seemed to be waiting for the right moment to completely envelop them, testing them with its probing reach every time they turned their backs on it. Maybe they would bump into another sewer dweller down here. What had the last one been talking about? Did she know something about Seb's mum? She was clearly crazy, so it probably didn't bear thinking about.

Seb increased his pace and caught up to Phulp. "So where are we going?"

"There are several long ladders down here that lead straight up to the wealthy part of the city above. We're heading to one of them. I have to warn you, it's quite a climb."

Seb thought about Gurt's knee and turned to look at him. The large Mandulu glared as if he'd heard his thoughts.

Seb smiled again before he replied to Phulp, "Sounds good to me."

After about another ten minutes, they came to a large open area. Unlike any other part of the sewer, it seemed to be a cave of some sort. Too dark to be certain, but when Seb looked across the space, he couldn't see a way out. "Um, Phulp, where's the ladder?"

But Phulp didn't respond as he strode forward.

When Seb looked behind at SA, he saw a look of unease on her face that reflected the feeling in his gut. "Phulp?" he said again.

Their tiny guide still didn't say anything.

This time, Gurt frowned at Seb, and Sparks seemed uneasy too as she scanned the area with her torch.

Phulp then stopped in the middle and turned to the group. The look on his face sat somewhere between resentment and regret.

It suddenly made sense when the shuffle of footsteps surrounded them, the acoustics of the cave amplifying the sound. When Seb looked back at the way they'd come in, he saw the tunnel blocked with silhouettes of figures. He spun on the spot and watched at least fifty Crimson foot soldiers emerge from the shadows around them. One final glance at Phulp and he heaved an exhausted sigh.

CHAPTER 39

S eb's pulse quickened as he spun on the spot to take in the Crimson soldiers who'd closed in around them. The need to run coiled within him, but no matter where he looked, he couldn't see anywhere to run to. He glanced back at their small and pale-skinned guide. "What have you done, Phulp?"

An insipid laugh squeezed from Phulp's white lips. "What does it look like I've done? Come on, Seb, you're a clever man. Surely you've worked it out by now?"

Any hope of escape Seb had vanished when he saw every robed foot soldier had at least one blaster in their hands. Even if they did fight them, and even if Seb could have avoided over fifty people firing at him—which he couldn't—the others wouldn't survive it. The faceless and silent guards continued to close in on them, the circle tightening like a strong grip around his throat.

When Seb looked at the others, he saw panic on Sparks' face. No doubt she represented how they all felt at that moment. It manifested on Gurt's features as anger. The brute looked like a Rottweiler chewing a wasp as he glared at the foot soldiers. SA, if anything, seemed even more serene than usual. Still and calm, her blue eyes shone in the darkness, her posture as impeccable as ever.

Other than the shuffle of their footsteps, the soldiers made no sound when they approached.

Phulp then spoke again, almost like he couldn't help himself. With his pudgy hands linked together in front of him, he laughed like before. "If it makes it any better, I'm sorry, I truly am."

To look at the smug albino-like creature wound Seb tight and he clenched his jaw. "You don't look sorry, you pale little rat."

"Now come on, Sebastian, there's no need for that kind of language, is there? The truth is, as much as I like you and your little band of mercenaries, nothing will ever compromise the love I feel for Mother. I owe Mother everything. She's the light on this dark planet of ours."

"The light that makes you slaughter your families?" Seb's voice echoed in the huge cave. A second later, the silence swallowed it and he saw Sparks look behind him, her already wide purple eyes wider still.

Before he'd even turned around, Seb knew who would be there. Although no amount of anticipation could prepare him for her.

At least nine feet tall, the huge cloaked mass stepped forward. As silent as the foot soldiers and as faceless, she moved closer to the group. Her red robe had been decorated with golden thread. It had to be the Crimson Countess. The woman's very presence seemed to suck the air from the cave, and even the foot soldiers froze when she walked past.

Just a few metres away from the group, the Countess raised her right hand. With one finger pointed at the sky, she spun it as if to signal for her soldiers to round her prisoners up.

Although it was impossible to tell, it seemed like the Countess looked Seb's way. He'd been the one to speak, after all. For a second, he glanced into the void inside her hood and shuddered.

The group put up no resistance when the foot soldiers bound their wrists. The soldiers then proceeded to take all of SA's knives, all of Gurt's guns, and Sparks' rucksack. They roughly patted Seb down, but when they found nothing, they backed away and shrugged at the Countess.

As the only voice in the cave, Phulp said, "It didn't matter how much you paid me, I would never betray Mother."

"Yet you still took our credits," Gurt said to the little creature.

A wide smile on his thin lips, Phulp nodded at the Mandulu. "Why, of course. I'm not going to pass up free credits, am I?"

None of the group replied to Phulp. The small rodent seemed far too pleased with himself already. They didn't need to validate his smugness any further.

The foot soldiers—headed by the huge robed figure of the Countess—walked from the cave back in the direction Seb and his group had come from. Hard to tell in the darkness, but it seemed like the only way out of the space.

With soldiers on every side, Seb felt their attention when it turned on him, even if he couldn't see a single face inside the hoods. Gurt led their line, SA in front of Seb, and Sparks behind him. All of them had their wrists bound together with a strange metal that had been wrapped around them like a huge bangle. Cold to the touch, the metal gripped too tightly for them to get out of.

Once they'd entered the tunnel they'd walked down to get to the cave, the soldiers around them thinned out a little. On such narrow walkways, they couldn't walk at the sides of the group even if they'd wanted to.

The small amount of time they'd spent in the cave had lowered Seb's guard against the reek of the tunnels. Now he'd re-entered them, he screwed his face up at the stench.

Several of the foot soldiers had flaming torches. They'd been scattered throughout the group, allowing them to light their way. The flicker animated the shadows and glistened off the damp rock beneath their feet.

Even in the warm orange glow of the flames, when a magnesium glare flared up behind him, it dazzled Seb. Everything slowed down as he listened to the *ching* of Sparks' broken metal cuffs when they hit the hard ground. Before the soldiers could react, she'd grabbed his right arm—her long fingers easily gripping his biceps—and dragged them both toward the frothy brown water.

Panic leapt through Seb's chest and into his throat as they fell toward the river of shit in slow motion, and before he could think about it, they'd broken the surface of the water with a loud *splash.*

Harder for having his hands cuffed, Seb rode the currents of the river and tried to stay afloat. When he looked behind at the blasters pointing their way, he ducked beneath the surface. He had his eyes closed, but still heard the volley of blaster fire hit the river above his head, and he still saw the flashes of light as the lasers shot past him.

The current beneath the surface seemed to run quicker than that above, and it dragged Seb away. The soldiers' shots went nowhere near hitting him.

Seb collided into a hard wall and fought his reaction to gasp. He kept his eyes so tightly closed, it hurt his face. The germs in the river would blind him if he opened them. Instead, he kicked his way to the surface, the current threatening to drag him away, and he looked back to where they'd come from.

The second Seb opened his eyes, he saw SA. Maybe Gurt looked at him too, but Gurt didn't matter at that moment. Not that she could hear him, but he said it anyway, "I'll be back for you, I promise."

The first of the soldiers seemed to notice Seb because a shot from a blaster hit the wall above him, sending chips of stone onto the top of his head. The fetid and muddy reek of excrement ran up his nose and he heaved before he ducked beneath the water again, pushed off from the wall he'd slammed into, and headed around the bend with the flow of the river.

CHAPTER 40

One of the longest days of Seb's life and it didn't look like it would be ending anytime soon. As he bobbed down the river of shit with Sparks at his side, he raised his head high enough above the water to keep the excrement away from his mouth.

Darkness surrounded them, and with every kick in the frothy water, Seb expected a tentacle to wrap around his ankle and drag him under. They still hadn't found a low enough walkway to allow them to climb out.

Fortunately, Sparks had been able to remove the metal around Seb's wrists when they'd gotten away from the soldiers, but other than that, they'd spent so much time in the rancid water that his skin had wrinkled and he could feel the waste from the residents of the city above soaking into his pores.

The splash of their movement gave the pair away to anyone who wanted to hear them as it called out in the darkness of the sewers.

When they came around the next bend, Sparks squealed and Seb's pulse spiked. Instead of seeing his little friend vanish beneath the surface of the water as he'd initially feared, he watched her swim to the opposite side of the river. When she climbed out, his heart lifted and he muttered, "Thank god."

However, before he moved over to her, a rush of water came down toward him. Something large seemed to have picked up their trail and plowed through the liquid towards them.

CHAPTER 41

The magnesium flash from Sparks' watch created a strobe effect as the pair of them sprinted through the pitch-black tunnels. Whether it did more harm than good, Seb couldn't tell. Each flash illuminated the way for a second but destroyed his night vision when the glare died down.

The *whoosh* of the beast in the river continued to chase them. When Seb glanced behind, he saw the monster's domed head break the surface of the water. Easily three times the size of the one they'd taken down earlier, its flaccid wings trailed behind it like a long tail. Hopefully the tightness of the sewers would restrict its movement should it try to fly.

The next flash from Sparks' watch and Seb saw it. "A ladder," he called after his small friend.

Sparks flashed her watch again. Only a step away from the rungs embedded in the wall, she leapt onto them and climbed.

Seb caught up a second later and followed her. Where the small Thrystian had been quick on her feet when she ran, her stature worked against her in scaling the ladder. Impatience tore through him as the rush of water closed in on them. Were Sparks not in front of him, then he'd be gone already.

After three or four metres, the ladder disappeared into a tunnel that led up through the ceiling. Although Sparks slipped up into the hole, Seb remained out in the open as the beast behind them rose from the river.

A glance behind as he climbed and Seb saw the cold fury in the monster's black eyes. As large as tank tyres, they fixed on him with a hatred that sent a shiver through him. This beast knew who'd taken the little one away from it, and it clearly had plans to make them pay.

Looking into a mouth three times the size of the one they'd seen earlier, Seb saw a horn-like beak inside it. It looked like it could shred metal. Like the little one, it had fleshy and torn strands of skin hanging down in front of its mouth. Covered in scars and cuts, the beast had the appearance of a creature used to battle.

The monster almost seemed to stand up on its tentacles as water rushed off its emerging form. Its large and jagged wings spread wide behind it as a wall of thin skin with elongated finger-like bones running through them. It roared, deeper and louder than anything Seb had ever heard before. The water bubbled around it from the vibration of the sound.

Just a metre from the tunnel above him and Seb willed his exhausted body up the ladder. He felt tempted to look behind at the beast one last time, but any more stalling and he wouldn't make it out of there. He used everything he had to climb, willing his tired legs and exhausted body up.

The wall next to Seb thundered as a thick tentacle crashed into it. The vibration damn near threw him to the ground, his wet hands struggling for grip on the metal rungs. But although he lost his footing, he managed to hold on. Just.

Seb scrabbled to find the rungs again with his feet as the beast behind him roared.

Before it could strike for a second time, Seb climbed up into the tunnel, the wall shaking again from another tentacle blow.

Seb continued on up behind Sparks. The tight space amplified their breaths as they exerted themselves. The wet *whoosh* of a tentacle reached up the tunnel after them.

The panic weakened Seb's legs, but just before the tentacle caught up with him, it stopped. He looked down to see the tip of it flap about as the beast tried to grab him, but it couldn't reach. Sparks looked down too.

"I think its tentacle's too thick to reach up," Seb said. The tip of the slug-like appendage thrashed wildly, hitting the walls in its snapping movement.

Sparks didn't reply; instead, she turned around and pushed on up the ladder. They needed to get out of the sewers now.

CHAPTER 42

The manhole cover at the top of the ladder made a loud screeching noise when Sparks shifted the heavy metal circle away from her. In anticipation of the flood of light, Seb squinted when he looked up. But no flood of light came. On the dark planet of Solsans, floods of light only happened when the slums below burned.

They'd climbed for at least fifteen minutes to get to the top of the ladder and the beast down below made sure they didn't forget it lay in wait for them. It roared and slapped the wall with its huge tentacles. It screamed. At one point, it made a deep booming sound that could have been a laugh.

When Seb finally crawled from the hole, he fell forward in an exhausted heap. Everything ached. His legs, his arms, his back, his lungs … Sweat dripped from him and mixed with the reek of sewage, running urine and excrement into his eyes no matter how many times he tried to wipe it away.

The top of the ladder brought the pair out into a quiet and foggy alleyway. A look up and down the street and they seemed to be alone.

The alley had been formed by a row of houses on either

side, and before Seb could catch his breath, Sparks stripped naked in front of him. Not knowing where to look, he did his best to stare into his friend's eyes. "What are you doing?"

"We stink."

"We do."

"And we need clean clothes."

"Also true."

"So that's what I'm doing. Keep a lookout, yeah?"

Before Seb could take the conversation any further, Sparks jimmied one of the house's windows open and slipped inside.

Wet, smelly, and now on his own in the strange city, Seb shivered in the cold and waited.

SPARKS RETURNED WITH AN ARMFUL OF CLOTHES FOR BOTH HER and Seb. She looked like she'd washed; her hair was cleaner and less matted than his, and her skin free of the flecks of excrement that no doubt coated his face. "The house is empty and they have running water," Sparks said. "Go inside and clean yourself up."

A risk, sure, but Seb needed to get himself clean. After another quick look up and down the shadowed and foggy alley, he climbed through the house's window into the darkness of the residence beyond.

A small amount of light came from what looked like the moon and some lamplight out in the street. It allowed Seb to see the drip of water Sparks had left behind her and he followed it through the house's living room to the bathroom.

The only running water in the slums came in the form of piss and shit in the streets. Up in the elevated city, they had plumbing in the first house they'd come across. It must be the same for every residence. Seb washed his face then stripped off and washed his body, the cold water making him shiver. Afterwards, he drank freely from the tap. The fresh water quenched his thirst and went a little way to easing the pain the smoke had caused his throat.

Because he hadn't taken the clothes with him that Sparks had brought out for him, Seb remained naked and left the house. He'd seen Sparks without clothes on; she could see him now. Not that she'd necessarily want to, but their friendship had probably passed that point.

After Seb climbed out of the window, Sparks—who'd dressed in what looked like a tan flight suit with more pockets than anyone ever needed—stared at him in horror.

Seb covered his modesty and said, "What?"

"Your clothes."

"I left them inside."

"I can see that. Look, I know the Countess will probably assume we're going to come for her, but do we need to leave a trail of breadcrumbs for her to follow?"

What an idiot. "I'm sorry, Sparks, I'm so tired, I wasn't thinking."

Sparks threw Seb his clean clothes and said, "Get changed and then get your other clothes out of there."

"What?"

"You *can't* leave them."

"But isn't it obvious that we've been here anyway? I mean, their window will be open—"

"Not if we close it."

"And their clothes will be missing."

"They may not notice that straight away. I guarantee you they'll find your stinking clothes on their bathroom floor within seconds though."

Half-dressed already, Seb continued to pull his clothes on and shook his head. "Damn it."

Once he'd got changed, he looked at Sparks. She'd folded her flight suit in many different places so it fit her. His, on the other hand, fit perfectly. As much as he wanted to ask his small friend to slip back into the house on his behalf, he'd made the mistake and he needed to rectify it. He looked back at the open window and sighed. "I won't be long."

SEB RETURNED TO THE HOUSE'S BATHROOM AND FOUND A towel to wrap his filthy clothes in. Once he'd tied the towel around the dirty garments, he stepped out into the front room and heard the lock click open on the front door. Muffled voices sounded on the other side. He couldn't hear what they said, but that didn't matter; what mattered was the owners of the house had returned home and the front door stood between Seb and his exit. If he ran for it now, they'd see him for sure.

CHAPTER 43

Seb withdrew into the bathroom and held his breath as he pulled the door shut. With a tight grip on the towel containing his stinking clothes, he pressed his ear to the wooden door to hear the beings on the other side. The cold atmosphere of Solsans had permeated the entire place and the door felt frigid to the touch, but he remained pressed against it.

The front door slammed shut and the footsteps of the residents padded around outside. They walked with little noise. From their sound, Seb would have assumed them to be tiny. But the fact that he'd found clothes his size suggested otherwise. A quick look at their bathtub and he confirmed it. No way were the residents any smaller than him. He looked down at his ridiculous flight suit full of pockets and shook his head. If anyone he knew saw him dressed like this …

"Can you smell that?" one of the residents said.

A different voice replied, a female by the sound of it. "What?"

"That smell. It smells like the drains again."

Seb held the clothes wrapped in the towel away from his

body as they dripped sewage water on the floor. Their damp weight tugged on his outstretched arm and he wanted to set them down to ease the ache, but to put them down would make him less ready to go. The opportunity to get out of there would come and he didn't need anything holding him back.

"I'll talk to the landlord," the first voice replied. The sound of his words got louder as he came closer to the bathroom door.

Seb drew a deep breath and the world around him slipped into slow motion. He held the towel in his left hand and clenched his right. Sometimes he had no other choice but to fight.

But instead of entering the bathroom, the steps continued past. Seb released a relieved sigh.

OVER THE NEXT FEW MINUTES, SEB LISTENED TO THE COUPLE on the other side of the door. At some point he would have to take the plunge and bust out of the bathroom to fight them. He couldn't wait forever. The creatures had come home now, so they probably wouldn't go out again. At present, he still had the element of surprise. Better he used that than be caught hanging out in their bathroom like a weirdo.

Before Seb could think on it any further, the *whoosh* of what sounded like igniting flames roared in the street outside.

"What was that?" one of the residents asked.

"Dunno," the other replied.

The front door clicked and the noise of something burning grew louder from where they'd clearly opened it. Hard to tell over the noise, but Seb couldn't hear the couple in the house anymore. They must have gone outside to investigate.

Seb yanked the bathroom door open and looked across the

living room. Candles had been lit and a table had been moved out into the middle of the room. Food of some description sat on it. Two meals ready for the two residents. He sprinted across the front room. It didn't matter if they saw him now, he had to get out of there.

When he got to the window, he saw the movement of purple eyes on the other side and Sparks flung it open. Tossing his towel of clothes through first, Seb followed them out by diving through the space and back out into the alleyway on the other side.

Outside, Seb panted, his breath visible in the cold air. He looked at Sparks. "What just happened?"

When Sparks didn't reply, Seb walked down to the end of the alley and peered around the corner. A small cottage with a thatched roof sat in a row of other houses. Its roof glowed with flames.

Upon returning to Sparks in the alleyway, Seb raised an eyebrow at her impish grin. She pressed a button on her wristwatch, which sent the same magnesium glare Seb had seen from it several times already.

A spark shot away from her and hit the pile of Seb's filthy clothes that he'd brought from the house. "Ain't technology grand?" she said as the ball of clothes went up in flames. "After you just went to all that trouble rescuing the clothes, the last thing we want to do is leave the pile here for someone to find."

"And you don't think the burning cottage will raise suspicion?"

"Nah. Thatched roofs and gaslights so close to one another is a recipe for disaster. I can't believe this is the first cottage to go up in flames." A quick look up the alley away from the end with fire and Sparks said, "Come on, let's get out of here."

Sparks led the way and Seb followed her, the plastic smell of his burning clothes behind them. "Sparks," Seb said.

The small Thrystian stopped and turned to him, her eyebrows raised as she waited for him to speak.

"That person in the sewers."

"The nutty woman with no hair?"

"Yeah. What did you think about that?"

"That she was a nutty woman with no hair."

"But she seemed to know."

Sparks walked off again and Seb fell into stride with her as he added, "She seemed to know about my mum."

"So, what, you think you're some kind of messiah now?"

It did sound ridiculous. Seb shrugged and stopped talking.

At the other end of the alley, Seb peered around the corner and his jaw fell loose. Instead of the same quaint scene of small houses and gaslight street lamps, there stood a huge spire that rose from a block of fog-enshrouded shadow. Jet black as if even the suggestion of light would be consumed by it, the stalagmite of a building shot from the ground and pointed straight up at the sky as if to curse the gods for its wretched existence.

The foggy shadow beneath the spire sat both as wide and as deep as a row of fifty small houses. When Seb looked up the craggy shaft for a second time, he struggled to see where it stopped and the pitch-black sky began.

A row of houses ran down either side of the dark palace. Despite the bizarre building next to them, the streets looked normal for the city, with street lamps and a wide road. The city dwellers wandered about as if they didn't have an enormous tower beside them more suited for hell than Caloon.

"Look at them," Seb said with a sneer, all of the people dressed in the ridiculous fashion that he and Sparks had been forced to adopt. "They walk around up here as if everything's normal and they don't have a care in the world. As if they have no awareness of the poverty and suffering below."

"While I agree with you," Sparks said, "I don't think feeling contempt for the people of this city is the way we should be going at the moment. I mean, in case you haven't noticed, there's a huge palace in the middle of the street. A palace that has Crimson Countess written all over it."

"That's got to be where the others have been taken," Seb said.

"And where my bag is," Sparks added.

Another look up the huge black spire and Seb nodded. "You're right. There's no getting away from what we have to do. Come on, let's go."

The pair of them stepped from the alley in the wide open space. A foreboding cold breeze hit Seb and his entire body tensed at its touch.

CHAPTER 44

A wide cobblestone square separated the alleyway from the palace. Black like the rest of the city, the road surface only revealed its undulations when Seb stood on it. It forced him to move slower than he would have liked for fear of turning an ankle. The full force of Solsans' bitter wind rushed across the open space and battered him. He hugged himself for warmth and spoke through a clenched jaw. "I feel like I'm getting hypothermia."

Sparks, seemingly impervious to the chill, ignored him.

Halfway across, Seb heard the sound of raised voices. He looked at the street that ran down the right side of the palace and saw a mob. Pitchforks would have completed their image. They held flaming torches and their faces were twisted with hate. They seemed to have someone in their midst that was the source of their ire.

Although many different species, the mob all had something in common. In the darkness of Solsans, their white skin shone so pale it almost glowed like Phulp's had. To even think about the small creature lifted bile into Seb's throat. *That little rat.*

The mob's skin stopped mattering when Seb saw their victim. Dressed differently to them in the clothes of a slum dweller, she couldn't have been any more than twelve years old. At first, the hate mob's angry protests swirled together as one bitter noise, but now they got closer, he heard their chants and yells. "Thief!" "Rat!" "Good-for-nothing!"

The girl's top rode up as they dragged her along the rough and cold ground. Too poor for a bra and too young to look like a woman anyway, she had the appearance of a skinny boy beneath her clothes. So malnourished, her concave stomach pulled into her lilac-skinned body with each heaving gasp as she cried. She fought against the tight grip one male had on her ankles with thrashing kicks, but he overpowered her with ease as he pulled her down the street.

Mostly males of their species, but also a few females, the crowd spat and kicked at the girl. "Thief!" "Scum!" One in every three kicks made the girl yelp like a broken and beaten animal.

Seb stopped, his stomach tense at the sight in front of him. Heavy breaths ran through him and the edges of his world blurred as his gift kicked in.

As if she'd sensed it, Sparks grabbed Seb's arm. When he looked down at her, he became conscious of his scowl and tried to soften his face.

"We can't do anything," she said in a low voice. "I hate watching this as much as you do." She pointed at the palace. "But we need to get in there to help SA and Gurt and get our target free. We fight now and it's all over."

The desire to argue burned in Seb's throat, but he saw the sense in Sparks' words.

Dressed like the rest of the citizens because of the clothes they'd stolen, Seb and Sparks were able to walk through the streets unnoticed. As harrowing as it felt to pass her by, they couldn't give up that advantage for one girl.

As they got closer, the male who dragged the girl lost his grip on her and she wriggled free. She made a break for it until another one of the mob kicked her legs away so hard that when she landed, her shoulder slammed against the solid ground with a stomach-churning *crack*. She cowered away from the mob and raised her arms up in front of her face as she screamed, "Please, I didn't mean to take it."

The male leaned over her, backed by the jeers of his pals. "You didn't mean to take it? The bread just jumped into your hands, did it?"

Snot and tears ran down the girl's lilac face. Half the size of the male, she looked up at him through glassy eyes. "Please, the bread had been thrown away. It was *stale*."

"It was *mine*. I didn't say you could take it."

"You'd thrown it *away*."

"And that's where it starts," he said. "You steal from the bin, and then you throw food away before it goes off so you can steal that too." The male's boot connected with the girl's stomach.

Her body wrapped around the impact with an *oomph*.

As she lay on the ground, she fought for breath, her slim form rocking with her gasping attempt.

Seb only realised he'd stopped again when Sparks tugged on his arm for a second time. Pain streaked up the sides of his face from where he locked his jaw tight. How could he walk away with the pack of bullies doing what they were doing? Older males and females, overfed and overprivileged, they treated the girl like she had invaded their world rather than lived on a planet they shared. Swollen with their own self-entitlement, they needed to be taught a lesson.

When an older female—frail-looking and so bitter she

seemed to be driven by the devil—stepped forward and kicked the girl in the face, Seb moved toward the mob again and Sparks tugged him back. She spoke to him through clenched teeth. "Don't lose your head."

Another male spat on the girl and kicked her. The girl's head snapped back at the impact and she fell limp.

It hurt Seb's heart to see the emaciated lilac-skinned girl knocked out on the ground. "You're telling me to walk away," he said to Sparks, "but you were hardly subtle when you set fire to that cottage."

"The difference is no one knows it was me. And, like I said, fires are bound to happen with gaslights and thatched cottages. You start a fight now and everyone will know who you are. We may be wearing the same clothes as them, but one look at our skin and it's pretty damn obvious we don't belong here."

The mob lifted the girl up above their heads and her small body hung limp, flopping about like a rag doll as they carried her away.

Seb remained rooted to the spot and watched them take the girl to the edge of the city. They counted down from three, and although it seemed obvious in hindsight, he didn't consider the horrific event until it happened.

On three, they launched her over the side.

Seb clenched his fists and turned on Sparks. "Did you just see that?"

Sparks tugged on his arm again and tears sat in her large purple eyes. "It's not that I don't care, Seb. I really do. I just know that we can't fight this fight."

As Sparks dragged Seb away, he continued to watch the privileged mob whoop and holler as they all stared over the edge of the city. He could catch them by surprise and shove at least half of them off after the girl before they defended themselves. But he didn't. He had to listen to Sparks. They behaved the way they did because the Countess allowed it. They had to get into the palace and cut the head off the snake.

The taste of bile still in his throat, Seb reluctantly turned away from the hate mob and followed Sparks toward the dark palace.

CHAPTER 45

As they got closer to the palace, Seb looked over at the hateful mob again. Most of them continued to peer over the side, obviously taking in every inch of the skinny girl's broken form. A strong enough gust of wind could send them all over after her. If only! He turned back around and shook his head. "I know we needed to walk away, but I don't like it. I don't like it one bit. She only took a loaf of bread."

"A loaf of bread her master had thrown in the bin," Sparks added.

"Right?"

"But we need to get SA and Gurt back. Were it just a case of rescuing a plummy toff from captivity, then I may have chosen the girl over our mission. But we need to make sure we get to our teammates as quickly as possible. Who knows what's happening to them. We kick off out here"—she pointed at the palace—"and it'll be a damn sight harder to get in there."

Tension balled in Seb's stomach from what he'd just witnessed, but he continued forward with Sparks and didn't look around again. The Countess would pay for running a city like Caloon.

The closer they got to the palace, the deeper the shadow it cast. So dark Seb almost expected to feel it cling to his skin like oil.

A few steps closer and two huge gates appeared from the shadows. Made from black wrought iron, they stood about ten feet tall. Instead of spikes along the top, they had what looked like forks. Each large prong had a barb on it like a fishhook. Once impaled on one, it would take a lot to get off it again.

Seb looked for a way in and seemed to notice it at the same time as Sparks said it.

"They're electric gates." Sparks scratched her face as she looked from one electric box to the other. They'd been affixed to the bottom of both posts.

"You think you can …?" But before Seb could finish, Sparks scuttled up to the gate and popped the front off one of the boxes.

Although Seb struggled to see into the foggy blackness beyond, it seemed unoccupied. He heard no movement, and the shadows—although dark—remained still. The hairs on the back of his neck rose as he waited for Sparks to do her thing and he continued to look for guards in front of them.

A sharp buzz and a flash of light punched from Sparks' corner of the gate. It temporarily blinded Seb. "Not very subtle," he said while rubbing his eyes.

"What do you want from me? We need to get in and I only have this watch."

A couple of loud *tocks* of a small engine willing itself into motion, and a *whir* called out as the gate slid open.

It creaked and groaned and Seb checked over both of his shoulders to see if anyone approached from behind. The lynch mob remained at the edge of the elevated section of the city, but apart from that, it seemed clear.

Once the gate had opened by a few feet, Sparks stood up and waved Seb over. "Come on," she hissed, "let's get inside. I reckon we have about fifteen minutes before the power comes back on."

Although not quite frozen to the spot, reluctance pulled Seb back for a second before he finally shrugged and followed his friend through the gap in the gate.

CHAPTER 46

Unable to see anything, Seb held Sparks' hand and kept up with her as best as he could. Somehow, the wide-eyed Thrystian seemed to be able to navigate the dark much more easily than him. She'd guided them into the palace and through some of the corridors, but he had no idea where they currently were. Without power, the inside of the palace had turned into a pitch-black void that seemed to leach the light from his eyes.

The ground, although uneven, didn't have any surprises to trip them up. At least, not yet anyway. The damp smell of the palace filled Seb's nostrils, forcing him to screw his nose up against the funk. He slowed down more with each step. When he'd pulled back to a walk, Sparks tugged his hand and hissed at him, "What are you doing? We don't have much time before the power comes back on."

"Sparks, without the power, we have nothing. We need to wait for it to come back on before one of us hurts ourselves. I'm totally blind and I can't imagine your sight's much better. We can't move in this darkness."

Sparks stopped completely and sighed. "You're right."

The shuffle of her feet called out and she pulled Seb with her until they came to a wall. "We'll wait for the lights to come back on."

Puffed out from the run and short of breath because of his rapid pulse, Seb leaned into the cold, damp wall and waited.

A MALE VOICE BURST FROM A SPEAKER SEB DIDN'T REALISE existed until it went off right next to him. He jumped to the side and his heart beat in his neck. He tried to blink the darkness away and stared in the direction of the sound. What at first appeared to be an echo turned out to be many speakers spreading away from them in both directions. The voice repeated the same order. "Mother requests your presence in the main hangar. You have three minutes."

A blink of light burst from above them, and Seb—still panicked from the loudspeaker—ducked as if the ceiling would fall on him. A flash more prolonged than the initial spark stabbed through the darkness, and then a light came on, illuminating the space where they stood.

Dazzled by the glare, Seb rubbed his eyes and looked around. The bright strip lighting in the ceiling lit up the place. The walls, which Seb expected to be damp black rock, were in fact gold. The cavernous space shone from the glare above.

When Seb finally worked out where they were, he turned to the stunned Sparks. "We're in the hangar."

Sparks nodded. "It certainly looks that way."

"The main hangar?"

"I would guess so."

"The one that Mother wants to meet them in?"

As Seb spoke, Sparks looked around as if searching for somewhere to hide. Instead of responding to him, she wrapped her long fingers in a constrictor's grip around his biceps. It stung as she dragged him into a small recessed area.

As they stood in the space, Seb pressed his back against the cold, hard wall. Condensation clung to the gold and soaked through his ridiculous outfit, but they seemed to be out of the way enough to remain hidden.

OVER THE NEXT FEW MINUTES, SEB AND SPARKS STAYED IN their small alcove and watched the place fill up with foot soldiers. A vast and cavernous room, the ceiling ran so high he expected to see clouds at the top of it.

A testament to the Crimson Countess' authority, the place had filled up within the three minutes she'd allowed her army to get there. Maybe all of them had turned up, maybe not, but Seb guessed at least two hundred of the red-robed creatures stood gathered in the hangar.

They all stared in the same direction and lined up with the smallest at the front and the largest at the back. At the very back stood two huge brutes. They looked to be at least thirty feet tall each and half as wide again. Their faces as hidden as the other soldiers, the wide creatures grunted and shifted as if the need for violence coursed through them. One blow from either of them would shatter a human skull. Even with his powers, Seb needed to avoid them.

A tall pillar of gold stood at the front of the room and seemed to be the focus of the foot soldiers' attention. Easily fifty feet from the ground, it looked out over the extravagant hangar. For all the poverty down in the slums, they had enough wealth lining the walls up here to ensure no creature on Solsans ever went hungry again.

When Seb saw the large, robed figure of what looked like

the Crimson Countess, he watched the entire room—even the beasts at the back—fall to their knees.

Silence swept across the place, and Seb's heart beat so hard he worried they'd hear it.

The Countess drew a deep breath and spoke to the crowd, her voice echoing through the extensive amphitheatre. "My children, you responded to my call."

"Yes, Mother," the entire room replied.

The loud response caught Seb off guard. He jumped and nearly yelled in surprise.

"You respect my power."

"Yes, Mother."

"You know how I love you all."

"Yes, Mother." Their collective response grew louder as if the mention of love invigorated them.

"You are mine; you serve me and I serve you. Together we run Solsans. We can be harsh, but fair. We bow down to the highest power."

"Yes, Mother."

The Crimson Countess spread her arms wide and shouted, "Foot soldiers, are you with me?"

The response this time seemed to shake the walls as every soldier roared, "Yes, Mother."

The chaos died down to near silence before the Countess spoke again. "Now, maybe I'm being paranoid, but the power never fails in this place."

Anxiety lurched through Seb's stomach. He chewed on his lip when he looked back out across the large gold cave. There didn't seem to be anywhere to run to should they discover them. They didn't exactly blend in either, in their ridiculous flight suits.

"Because of that," the Countess said, "I want this place searched from top to bottom for intruders." She slammed a clenched fist against her large open palm and called out again, "If there's anyone in here, we'll damn well find them."

The foot soldiers all jumped to their feet. As one, they clenched their fists and pressed them together. They bowed to their leader. When they straightened back up, they yelled, "Yes, Mother!"

Seb looked at Sparks and he saw true fear in her wide purple eyes. What had they got themselves into?

CHAPTER 47

Seb looked for somewhere to go. Anywhere that got them out of the small recess next to the army paying homage to Mother would have been good. But the second they stepped from the alcove, one of the foot soldiers would surely see them.

Before Seb could think on it any further, he jumped at the sharp sting in his ribs. When he looked down, he saw Sparks with her pointy little elbow dug into his side. Were it not for the hangar full of soldiers then he might have yelled out; fortunately he had the presence of mind to keep his mouth shut. While rubbing the pain of her jab, he scowled at her as if to say, *What?*

Sparks pointed with one of her long fingers.

Following her intention, Seb shook his head and spoke in a whisper. "No way."

The chant of "Mother! Mother! Mother!" came from the hangar. Seb shook his head at Sparks again just to be sure she'd understood his intention.

To continue their silent conversation, Sparks shoved her

hands inside one of the many pouches in her adapted suit and removed the memory stick Moses had given them.

"Where did you hide that?"

Before Sparks could respond, Seb raised a halting hand at her. "Actually, don't answer me."

Seb saw the bank of computers almost as soon as the lights had come on in the place. But to get to them, they'd have to expose themselves. It would be madness to even try. There had to be other computers somewhere. They could use them.

Crouching down so he could be at Sparks' level, Seb said, "Have you seen how many soldiers there are out there? No way can we get across to that machine unnoticed."

"But have you seen what's hanging up next to it?" Sparks asked.

Another look at the bank of computers and Seb saw it for the first time. "A robe."

"A selection of robes."

"But it doesn't look like they have any small enough for you."

Where most crowds would have waned, the group of fanatics out in the hangar continued to punch their fists together and chant for their mother.

Without another word, Sparks sprinted from Seb's side and ran for the robes. He reached out to grab her, but she'd gotten away too quickly. As the calls in the hangar rang out, he watched his little friend move like the wind. It would test the zealousness of the Countess' army. If they remained fixed on their leader, they wouldn't notice Sparks. They certainly sang a convincing tune.

Upon reaching the robes, Sparks jumped and kicked off a wall. Seb saw her foot slip, but she still managed enough propulsion to grab the robe, yank it from the peg, and land silently with it in her grip.

Sparks sprinted back across the gap with the robe trailing behind her, and still the chants from the army continued on.

Skidding to a stop next to Seb, Sparks held the robe up at him. "Here you go."

Unsure whether to laugh or shout at her, Seb only realised just how badly he shook when he reached out to take the garment.

"I'll stand on your feet when you walk," Sparks said.

"Sweet, like a little child?"

Sparks scowled at him and showed him her watch. "Remember how painful this electricity bolt is ... especially when it hits the most sensitive parts of the body." A vicious smile spread across her face as she looked at Seb's crotch.

"Just get on my feet," Seb said and wrapped her up in the robe.

The cloak clearly hadn't been washed since the last soldier wore it because Seb could smell the reek of sweat and something else. It reminded him of a dirty dog, and it took a few seconds of concentration to make sure he didn't vomit.

THE CHANTS FROM THE SOLDIERS WENT ON FOR ANOTHER FIVE minutes at least. The Crimson Countess stood on her platform and continued to watch her adoring legion below before she finally said, "Okay, my children, you know what to do. Search every inch of this place."

Ever alert, Seb had been waiting for this moment and he carefully watched as the army dispersed. When he guessed it to be at its most chaotic, he stepped out into the crowd of soldiers and joined the hustle and bustle.

Seb's thudding pulse accompanied his every step. Sparks weighed heavier on his feet than he expected. Tempted to look around, he resisted the urge and walked over to the computer with purpose.

No one bothered him, so when he got to it, he popped his robe open at the front and showed Sparks the machine. He only saw her long fingers as they stretched out with the small memory stick in a pinch. Once she'd plugged it into the slot, her hands moved like lightning over the keys.

Heavy thuds approached and Seb cuffed Sparks around the side of the head. She tapped the keyboard several more times before she pulled back into his robe and he did the buttons up.

The large soldier peered over Seb's shoulder at the computer's screen. His voice sounded like a rockslide. "What are you doing, brother?"

"Um ..." Seb shook when he turned around and stared up into the dark hood of his interrogator. "I'm ... um." He looked back at the screen to see a schematic of the palace. "I'm just checking to see all the cells are locked. I'm worried the power cut may have shorted some of the gates and freed them. Maybe that was why someone cut the power in the first place."

Heavy breaths rocked the large Crimson soldier and he kept his attention on Seb. Fire flushed Seb's cheeks as he stared into his interrogator's dark hood. If he couldn't see the foot soldier's face, then the foot soldier wouldn't be able to see his either.

The foot soldier finally said, "Fine. You do that and follow up anything suspicious, okay?"

Seb nodded.

After the soldier had walked away, Seb reached down and undid his robe again. "Right, Sparks, hurry it up, yeah?"

It only took Sparks a few more minutes before she unplugged the memory stick, withdrew her hands, and tapped Seb's knee. He just barely heard her soft voice say, "All done."

Seb did his robe up, looked around to be sure he hadn't attracted any unwanted attention, and walked away from the computer and the hangar.

CHAPTER 48

Sparks might have been small, but after a few minutes of carrying her, Seb felt like she weighed a ton. A grimace locked his face tight and he pushed through the pain of her on his feet. The bones along the top of them felt like they could snap at any moment. One foot in front of the other, he walked down the dingy tunnels, directed by his small friend.

In a dark and dank corridor, the cave walls as black as the floor and strip lighting running overhead, Seb heard footsteps coming his way.

When Sparks said, "Keep going," Seb cuffed her around the side of the head.

The little troll stamped down on his foot just as a group of Crimson soldiers came into view. A clenched jaw helped Seb keep his reaction in and he pulled his robe closed to hide Sparks.

The band of four soldiers walked past, all four of their faces hidden in shadow, and all four of them staring straight ahead. If they looked at Seb, they didn't make it obvious.

Once they'd gone from view, Seb cuffed Sparks around

the side of the head again. He'd be lying if he said he didn't enjoy antagonising her.

Sparks poked her head from Seb's robe and looked up at him. "Will you *stop* doing that?"

"How else am I to alert you to the soldiers?"

"A little nudge'll do it."

"You've never been hit before, have you, Sparks?"

"I'm too smart to get hit."

Seb cuffed her around the head again and couldn't help but laugh.

When she flashed her electrocuting watch at him, Seb raised his hands. "Okay, okay. Sorry. I'm in so much pain with you on my feet that I have to let it out somehow."

"It's not like I can walk though, is it? Unless you have a small robe I don't know about?"

"I know. So where are we going?" Seb said.

"Keep heading straight down this corridor. We're nearly there."

Seb didn't respond as he continued to walk. Instead, he looked at the cavernous tunnel, centuries old and spoiled by the strip lighting. White cables ran throughout the entire place. Although, better to have the aesthetics spoiled than not be able to see where they were going.

"These tunnels remind me of home."

Sparks looked up at him but didn't respond.

"We used to have smuggling caves on Danu. They hadn't been used for centuries, so the government turned them into a tourist attraction. We went to see them on a school trip. They scared the life out of me as a boy; I believed all kinds of monsters lived in them."

The sound of more soldiers stamped toward them. Seb stopped himself short of cuffing Sparks and hissed, "Hide."

Like the others, the soldiers passed without batting an eye. They spoke when spoken to and followed orders.

Once they'd moved on, Seb tapped Sparks on the side of her head and she pulled his cloak open again.

"Turn right," Sparks said.

Seb hadn't seen it until she'd given him the direction, but when he looked right, he saw a tunnel branch off from the main one and headed for it. Every step took more effort than the last and he breathed heavily as he plodded forward, his legs slowly turning to lead.

When they came to a door, Sparks burst from Seb's robes. "This is it."

Exercising caution where she hadn't, Seb looked both up and down the corridor to make sure they were alone. It seemed clear.

Although Sparks had her watch ready, when she pushed the door handle down in front of her, it swung open. A half smile lifted her face. "Wow, I wonder why they haven't locked it."

"Maybe they feel confident in their ability to stop intruders?" Seb said.

"I hope that's it and it's not a trap. We'll have an easy ride if that's the case."

Even though Sparks had hopped off his feet, Seb still felt both the impressions of her heels and the fatigue in his muscles. "Easy for who?"

But Sparks didn't answer and Seb followed her into the room.

Much like the room on *The Black Hole,* the space they entered had been stacked with confiscated items. Crates leaned against the walls and stood from ground to ceiling in the middle of the space too. A small pathway had been left unobscured to allow access to everything. "How the hell will we find your stuff in here?"

A press of her watch and a low-pitched whistle sounded out. Sparks followed the noise and Seb followed Sparks. She pressed her watch again and something made the same noise. He followed her again.

One more press and Sparks came to the shortest stack of crates in the room. Her bag rested on top of it and both Gurt's blasters and SA's knives sat beneath it.

Seb quickly removed his heavy robe. Where he'd been sweating beneath the thick cape, he now shivered. "I'm glad it's cold in here"—he looked down at the robe—"I was boiling up beneath that bloody thing."

Hunched down by her bag and rummaging through it, Sparks pulled out her mini-computer then hooked it up to her watch with a cable.

Just holding SA's knives set Seb's heart aflutter. Although he'd been around her when she'd used them, it didn't seem appropriate to ask to look at them. They seemed too personal. But now, with the beautifully carved ivory handles and the filigreed blades in his possession, he could properly take them in.

"Come on," Sparks said.

As Seb slipped Gurt's and SA's harnesses on, he felt the collective weight of both the blasters and the knives and rolled his shoulders to try to find some comfort.

After Sparks passed Seb his robe, she darted across the room. When she came back with a crimson robe of her own, Seb heaved a relieved sigh. The weight of the weapons would be much easier to bear now he didn't have to carry her too.

With both of them loaded up and ready to go, Seb paused for a moment, the smell of leather coming from the two harnesses. "I can't help but feel like we're being set up."

Sparks shrugged. "We can't deal with what we don't know. We'll just have to wait and see what happens." She lifted her small computer up. "I've transferred all the data over to this. It'll be easier to follow it now, so we should get through here quicker. We can't worry about anything other than the now. I know you have a bad feeling, but I think we might just do this."

And with that, Sparks led the way out of the small storeroom.

CHAPTER 49

Sparks seemed to have energy to burn as she streaked off ahead of Seb. Although if he'd been carried from the hangar like she had, he'd probably have the same zest for moving on too. Weighed down with SA's and Gurt's weapons, he lagged behind, but at least the stark lighting in the hallway allowed him to keep focused on his little friend up in front.

Without missing a beat, Sparks took a sharp left turn and Seb listened to the echo of her light steps as she disappeared down what sounded like a stairway.

When Seb stopped at the top of the steep stairs and looked down to see Sparks disappear into the dungeon-like darkness below, he nearly didn't follow her.

Before Sparks vanished from view, she looked back up at him, her face hidden in the hood's shadow. "Come on," she said and turned the glowing screen of her small computer for Seb to see—not that he could. "They're down here."

"Think of SA," Seb muttered to himself before he shook his head and followed Sparks.

TWO SOLDIERS STOOD IN FRONT OF A LARGE WOODEN DOOR AT the bottom of the stairs. Both of them lifted their chests and raised their blasters.

Before they could speak, Sparks said, "We've been sent down to check on the prisoners."

"Why?" one of the soldiers replied in a gruff voice as he stepped toward them.

"Since the power cut, Mother wants us to check *everywhere*."

"But other than the lights, there's nothing reliant on power down here."

"Do *you* want to tell her that?"

The shadowed face of the foot soldier stared at Sparks for a moment before he stood aside and unlocked the heavy door for them.

Sparks walked through and Seb followed on her heels with his head raised. Even if he didn't feel confident, he needed to project it.

The stench damn near knocked Seb over. Worse than the streets in the slums, worse even than the sewers they'd gone through to get into the elevated city, it reeked of both human waste and a rich funk of rotting flesh.

Seb gagged several times and his mouth dried from the heat in the room. A sharp look from Sparks and he finally managed to pull himself together.

The same lights that ran along the corridor's ceilings ran along the dungeon's ceiling. Although they had far fewer in the dungeon. As a result, many parts of the cave were sunk in deep shadow. Unfortunately, some of the dungeon remained all too visible.

In the centre of the room—lit up as if beneath an inter-rogator's spotlight—a wooden structure the size of a bed had a small female strapped to it. About the same size and shape of a human child, she had scaly green skin. On closer inspec-tion, Seb recognised the device as a rack. The small child looked like she should have been smaller. Her tiny form stretched beyond a point it should be able to. Dead from the process, her mouth hung open and her lifeless eyes stared at nothing.

In front of the rack sat a large wooden chair. The slumped form of an older female sat strapped to it. She had the same scaly green skin of the stretched girl. Seb would have also taken her to be dead were it not for the gentle rocking motion as she sobbed in near silence.

Sick to his stomach, Seb walked over to her and undid the straps on the female's arms and feet. So what if the soldiers looked in? They couldn't leave her like that.

Once he'd freed her—the female smelling as bad as the dungeon itself—she simply remained in the chair. A fogged glaze sat in her eyes as if she'd lost her mind. Seb stared at her face for a few more seconds and saw the familial resem-blance. She was the mother of the dead girl for sure. "Damn," he whispered, his hushed tones rippling away from him.

Seb didn't have time to do more than he'd done, so he spun around and took the room in. Although dark in there, his eyes adjusted to the poor light and he saw various torture devices dotted around him. Rather than getting used to the funk of the place, it seemed to get worse as he looked at the tools designed to cause pain. Each one had been stained with the blood of many victims. Rusty, dirty, and sharp, they'd all been created with agony in mind. They'd kill beings through either spearing them, stretching them, or hanging them. Half of them still had the broken forms of dead victims on them, and whilst some of the remains looked fresh, some were rotted beyond recognition.

Short and sharp breaths ran through Seb and the room seemed to get hotter. When he looked into the corner, he saw something boiling there. It added to both the heat and the stench in the room, but he didn't want to investigate it.

Along one wall ran a line of cage doors. Bodies shuffled inside, and when one of the creatures within stepped forward, Seb gasped. Sparks looked up from her mini-computer and he nodded in the direction of the cages. "The child soldiers. Sparks, look."

Sparks looked across the dungeon at the cages full of young males. Still unable to see her face, Seb read her mood from her utter stillness. What could she say to that? If they released the boys before they found Gurt and SA, the commotion it would undoubtedly cause could mean they'd never get their friends back.

A long finger protruded from Sparks' robe and she pointed away to another corner of the dungeon. "Over there. Gurt and SA are over there."

With the map in her hands, Sparks led the way again. Seb followed, watching the caged boys for a little longer before he focused ahead. When he caught up with Sparks, he found her in an empty cage. She stared down at her screen. "The map says they should be here. They should be locked in this cage."

Seb looked back out into the central area of the dungeon and his heart sank. "Uh, Sparks," he said as he pointed into the darkness.

Sparks came to Seb's side and heaved a weary sigh. "Oh no."

Silhouetted in the dark, Seb looked at the limp and

hanging forms. One large brute of a creature, the other, a slim and slender female. He shook his head as the strength in his legs ebbed away. With a hand on the wall, the surface hot and damp to the touch as if the stone sweated, Seb said, "I can't believe we didn't get to them in time."

CHAPTER 50

"We have to cut them down," Seb said as he walked toward the forms. His voice warbled when he spoke again. "I can't believe we didn't get here in time."

The two limp bodies each had a hood over their face. They'd clearly been put on before they'd hanged them because the rope bunched the fabric around their necks.

Seb removed one of SA's knives from her harness. He got to Gurt first. It would be easier to see him dead than it would SA. His hands shook as he sliced into the Mandulu's hood.

The second the brown sack fell open, Seb let out a relieved sigh. "It's not him, Sparks." A look at the bloated face, the weight of the creature's body pulling against the tight noose around its neck, and he laughed as he stared into the brute's bulging eyes. "He's too pretty to be Gurt."

"Even when I'm missing, you're rude about me."

Seb spun around to see the large form of Gurt emerge from the shadows. The blue bioluminescent glow of SA's eyes stepped out of the darkness with him and Seb's heart skipped.

Before he'd thought about it, Seb rushed over and held

both of SA's hands as he stared into her brilliant glare. He wanted to hug her, but he refrained. "Oh my. Are you okay?"

Instead of her often blank expression, the slightest hint of a smile played on SA's lips before she nodded.

"I'm fine, by the way," Gurt said.

The brief flash of happiness returned to impassivity on SA's serene face, and she dragged a man forward from the dark.

With long dirty hair and a scraggly beard, he walked with a limp. Seb stared at the mess of a man. "George Camoron?" After a few seconds, he looked at both Gurt and SA. "Why's he still gagged? And why are his hands still tied together?"

SA shoved the man forward and Seb removed his gag, screwing his nose up at his dirty stench.

"My god, why have you taken *so* long to get to me? Do you know how long I've been down here? Do you know who I *am*?"

Before he could say anything else, Seb pulled the gag back across the man's mouth. Because he still had his hands tied behind his back, the plummy excuse of a being couldn't do anything about it. Seb nodded at both Gurt and SA. "Okay, I understand now."

Despite silencing the man, Seb dragged him forward into the little light they had down in the dungeon. Almost unrecognisable from his picture, his hair had grown long, his skin had turned a few shades darker because of dirt and sweat, and he'd lost a lot of weight. Dressed in what looked to be the suit he'd probably arrived in several years ago, the black fabric that remained of it hung from him in scraps. His crusty trousers seemed to be stained with his own waste and blood.

Just to touch the man made Seb want to wash, but they had to get him out of there. As he turned Camoron around, dread sank through Seb's form. The back of his clothes had been ripped to shreds. The white fabric of his shirt had been stained with old yellow blood, and angry white scars were raked down his back as if he'd been mauled. "My *god*," Seb said, "what have they done to you?"

The lights in the dungeon suddenly grew so bright Seb couldn't see. Regardless of his temporary blindness, he heard the voice of the soldier with crystal clarity. "Nothing compared to what we're going to do to you."

CHAPTER 51

I took a few seconds for Seb to recover his vision from the glare, but when he did, he saw the two soldiers they'd persuaded to let them into the dungeon and a whole host more behind them. The narrow doorway only allowed a few through at a time. The hallway on the other side appeared to be crammed with red cloaks too. An image of the hangar they'd been in earlier and the sheer number of soldiers in there ran through his mind. It wouldn't be easy to get free.

Seb pulled George Camoron behind him, and although he should have focused on their enemy, he couldn't help looking around the dungeon now the lights had been turned up. The child on the rack looked more horrendous, her shoulders and hips fully dislocated. The kid's mother remained slumped in her seat, as inconsolable as before.

The prisons with the boy soldiers in them were huge. A few hundred adolescents were packed into each one, maybe more. Thousands of boys in total, they all stared from the cages at the commotion outside.

The soldier that had spoken seemed confident the five

wouldn't get out. Instead of fighting them straight away, he walked over to a girl who'd been tied to the wall. No more than seven years old, the small creature had the familiar pasty tinge common with Solsans' residents. The lack of sunlight turned everyone pale. She had long red hair, two horns poking through it, and a large protruding bottom jaw full of jagged teeth.

Delirious with the suffering she'd endured, she seemed oblivious to the soldier, who walked over to her and pointed at where her right arm should be, now just a bloody, cauterised stump. The soldier smiled. "This is what we do to thieves. She stole a cabbage from the ground."

Although her blue eyes rolled in her head, the girl managed to rouse herself, looked at the soldier, and spoke with slurred words. "It had been thrown away. It was *rotten*."

The soldier spun on her and screamed in her face, "You *stole* it!"

The boys in the cages recoiled at his loud accusation amplified by the acoustics of the cave. Conditioned to fear their masters, the violent outburst clearly triggered something in them.

The soldier then lifted her other hand. The tips of her fingers had been shaved away and they glistened with blood. "We're taking the other arm now." He laughed. "An inch at a time."

The girl's head dropped and she slumped against the restraints holding her up. She didn't look like she'd make it to the end of her other arm.

Seb might not have been able to see the soldier's face, but he could hear the smile in his words. "If this is what we do to common thieves, imagine what we'll do to you lot."

The edges of Seb's vision blurred. When his world slipped into slow motion, he discarded his crimson robe. He then undid the harnesses with both Gurt's blasters and SA's knives on them and tossed them to the pair. He shoved George Camoron even farther away. The fool stumbled and fell over.

Before the soldier could draw his blaster, Gurt slipped one of his own free and pulled off two shots, dropping the soldier and his mate.

More of them rushed forward as a red tide. The bottleneck slowed them down and gave SA the chance to cross the dingy room toward the boiling pot in the corner.

With everything slowed down, Seb saw the body—or at least what remained of the body—sat in the pot. Green skin that looked duller than it should be, the process of boiling it clearly leeched the colour from the now pale flesh. The black metal cauldron sat on a bed of hot coals.

One swift kick and SA launched the pot and many of the coals at the door. The scalding water smothered the first few soldiers, who screamed at the contact, and several of the coals burned into their cloaks.

With the plastic smell of burning robes in the air, Seb looked at the remains of the green creature as it lay flopped on the ground, almost unrecognisable as anything once living.

The soldiers at the door screamed louder as they continued to burn. Gurt looked at both Seb and Sparks and then said, "What are you two wearing?"

Seb looked down at the tan-coloured monstrosity.

"There's so many pouches," Gurt said, "it looks like it would take you twenty minutes to find your keys."

"They all wear this kind of crap out there," Seb said. "It helped us move through the city without standing out."

Gurt raised an eyebrow at Seb. "I'll be honest, I'm a little bit embarrassed to be seen with you looking like that, but we can't do anything about it now, can we? I suppose we'd best get out of this crappy dungeon and away from here."

As Gurt spoke, more and more soldiers flooded into the basement. The large Mandulu ground his jaw so his horns pushed up his face and he ripped off several more blasts. He then led the way from the dungeon and the others followed.

CHAPTER 52

Gurt strode towards the guards with a blaster in each hand, his guns bucking every time he shot one. SA followed after him, her polished blades blinking beneath the glare of the now brightly lit room.

After a deep breath, Seb moved off too. They'd been on the go since they'd landed on Solsans and he felt exhausted. His entire body ached and his sore limbs threatened to stop working, but he gritted his teeth and pushed forward.

The narrow stairway only allowed Gurt and SA to fight side by side. Useless as he stood behind them, Seb ran over to one of the cages with the boys in it instead.

Wide eyes stared from the dark. Too scared to speak, the pale creatures pulled away from the door. They huddled together in the shadows at the back. A large padlock clamped their gate shut. So large, Seb had to grab it with both hands and pull. It did little to remove it from the cell door.

When Seb looked behind, all of his team had vanished, but he could hear them fighting on the stairs.

Seb noticed a rack of metal spikes to his right. He grabbed one—the shaft tacky with old blood—and pulled. At first, the spear didn't budge. With his right foot pressed against the rack to stop it moving, he clamped his jaw and pulled again.

Several yanks later it came free with a loud tearing sound. The pole—although hollow—seemed strong enough. Seb turned the weapon around so the pointy end poked up at the dungeon's ceiling. He gripped it with both hands, focused on his target, and drove the butt of the weapon against the large padlock. He scored a direct hit, but the pole simply bounced off it. A combination lock, the soldiers who'd know the code now lay dead on the ground by the exit to the dungeon.

"Come on, Seb," Sparks called from somewhere up the stairs. "We can't hang around any longer. We need to get out of here."

Exhausted and running out of ideas, Seb screamed through his clenched jaw as he drove another heavy blow against the huge lock. A spark of metal on metal, but the lock remained clamped shut.

The same alarm Seb had heard when he'd been in the hangar with Sparks rang out. A female voice called through the cavernous palace. The echoes of chaos rushed down into the dungeon and he could just about make out her words. "All units head to the dungeon right now. Escaped prisoners. Neutralise by using all force necessary. All units …"

"Seb," Sparks called again and she appeared in the dungeon doorway, "we need to get the hell out of here. This is our window."

A look into the cell and the boys continued to stare at Seb. Their saviour, he now had a choice to make. Him or them.

A lump rose in his throat and regret twisted his spirit.

One last look at the boys and Seb ran off after Sparks.

CHAPTER 53

The narrow stairs that led up and out from the dungeon only allowed room for Gurt and SA to fight their way through. Nearly at the top now, Seb, Sparks, and the rich idiot followed slowly behind. They moved one step at a time as the dark stairwell lit up with sounds of blaster fire, expletives, and the squelch of knives cutting flesh.

The corridor at the top of the stairs seemed clear for now. Well, other than the pile of dead foot soldiers. Guilt, fatigue, and his generally poor fitness all dragged Seb down, but he couldn't stop now. The alarm continued to shriek through the hallways of the palace, and the annoying woman repeated the same order to get to the dungeon.

"Which way?" Gurt called at Sparks, his blasters raised and ready to use.

Sparks stared at her mini-computer before she pointed down the corridor. "That way."

When the stampede of soldiers' footsteps came from the direction she pointed in, Sparks quickly pointed the other way. "That way."

Faster than the lot of them, Sparks took off at a sprint. SA followed on her heels while Seb ran in the middle, dragging the stupid toff with him. Gurt took up the rear.

The sound of Gurt's blasters went off, and when Seb turned around, he saw the bolts fired from them light up the dark corridor. They took out four Crimson soldiers. Gurt released several more shots as more of the soldiers came into view.

Seb had seen Sparks run and knew she could move faster, but she'd slowed her pace so they could stay together. The backlight on her computer's screen lit up from the map on the display.

Every few seconds, Gurt released another volley of blaster fire. George Camoron flinched with every shot. As much as Seb didn't want to give the privileged idiot the benefit of the doubt, he looked like he'd been through hell. Were Seb in his position, then his nerves would undoubtedly be shot to pieces too.

"Get in," Sparks called back.

Seb dragged the rich idiot into the dark shadow of a wall. As they stood there, George Camoron breathed as if on the edge of a panic attack, and Seb came close to knocking him out to keep him quiet.

Before he could react, a group of soldiers tore past them. They'd come from the direction the gang were heading in, and in their haste to get to what Seb assumed to be the dungeon, they didn't notice the five figures in the cover of the shadows. The group set off again before the ones behind caught up.

Several twists and turns and Sparks led them to the large, open space of another hangar. Unlike the one they'd been in when the Countess gave her rousing speech, this one had some use. It had ships everywhere. The ground continued as the same black rock, but the walls were lined with chrome. The place seemed abandoned.

Gurt, clumsy with his wobbly gait—his damaged knee obviously making it harder for him—ran in as the last of the group members. Sparks tapped on her computer screen and the large doors whirred to life as they slowly closed.

It sounded like a hundred guards were chasing them up the hallway, and the large doors couldn't close quickly enough. None of the foot soldiers had appeared yet, but Gurt shot through the decreasing gap down the hall anyway. The approaching noise of soldiers seemed to slow in response to the warning shot.

The first few foot soldiers came into view and SA rushed over to be next to Gurt. She threw several of her knives at them. Despite the distance of at least twenty metres, every one of her blades scored a direct hit. They disappeared inside the shadowed hoods of the soldiers and Seb watched them fall a second later. He couldn't help but smile to himself as he recovered his breath from the run.

Once the doors had fully closed, Sparks used her watch to blow up the control panel. It lit up and belched bursts of fire and electricity before the life left it. "That should hold them for a short time," Sparks said.

The gang, led by Sparks, ran across the hangar to the closest ship, their stamping feet echoing in the large space. When Seb noticed a collection of ships in one corner, he said, "Isn't that …?"

Gurt looked over. "The ships they used to bomb the slums."

"So they did it to their own people?" Seb asked. "But why?"

"To give them a common enemy," Camoron said. "If they

see the Countess protecting them, they'll get behind her cause much more readily."

"Wow," Seb replied. "I thought I'd already seen the worst that woman could do to her citizens."

A haunted look stared back at him from Camoron's withdrawn face. "I don't know what you've seen, but my guess is that you've not even scratched the surface."

A chill snapped through Seb as they ran up the ramp into the ship. A few seconds later, the engine roared to life and Sparks had them off the ground.

Seb ran to the cockpit and looked through the windshield. "Why are the doors still closed, Sparks?"

The small Thrystian shook her head and tapped her small computer. "I don't know. They should be opening."

The ship rocked from side to side as it hovered in the air and the sound of blaster fire crashed against the other side of the hangar doors from where the soldiers were trying to burst in.

"It'll have to be done manually," Sparks said.

With SA in the co-pilot's seat and Gurt's bad knee, Seb said, "What do I have to do?"

Sparks looked at Seb for the briefest moment and didn't reply.

"Come on, Sparks, we don't have time to mess around."

A nod and Sparks held her screen up. Four numbers appeared on it. "Zero, seven, one, two. You need to put that code into the box by the door. Not only will it open the doors for us, but it will disable all of the Countess' tracking systems. It'll make it much harder for them to follow us." She then pulled an earpiece from her bag and gave it to Seb. "This will help us communicate while you're out there."

As Seb clipped the earpiece to his right ear, he looked at SA and met her wide and compassionate gaze. If he needed motivation to go, she'd just given it to him. "Zero, seven, one, two," he said.

Just before Seb left the ship, he grabbed Gurt. Aware of the scrutiny from the others, he leaned in and whispered in the Mandulu's ear. When he pulled back, Gurt glared at him.

"And rest that knee up, old man," Seb said.

Gurt scowled even harder than before.

Before Gurt could reply, Seb jumped off the ship into the hangar.

CHAPTER 54

The earpiece clung to Seb's ear, yet he still pressed against it to make sure it didn't fall out. He didn't have time to go back to get it if that happened. The sound of blaster fire battered the doors separating the hangar from the rest of the palace. The large steel barrier seemed to be stronger than the attack levelled at it. For now.

The ground in the hangar looked like the rest of the palace. Black and uneven, it had been flattened enough that Seb could run across it without fear of tripping. The chrome walls had fuel ports down each side at regular intervals. They also had spaces to hold tools, and cupboards for flight suits. The palace had been set up to run a fleet of ships. A small fleet, but a fleet nonetheless. When the Crimson Countess only ever fought her own ships in the sky, why would she need anything more?

By the time Seb had crossed the hangar, the sound of blaster fire against the locked door had ceased. Instead, he heard something much worse: the buzz and crackle of a blowtorch. He looked around to see the white-hot glow as the torch ate through the metal. It wouldn't be long before they cut through the door and the Crimson foot soldiers spilled into the hangar.

"You're looking good, Seb," Sparks said in his ear, and Seb turned around to look at the ship as it hovered and wobbled in mid-air. The small Sparks gave him a large thumbs-up.

At the control panel to the hangar door they intended to escape through, Seb said, "Zero, seven, one, two, right?"

"Zero, seven, one, two," Sparks repeated.

A hole opened up in the large doors holding the Crimson soldiers back. Molten steel dripped from it like snot. Seb's hand shook as he tapped the silver buttons on the numeric keypad. He then pressed the green tick and the motors in the large doors whirred and thunked.

As the door opened, Seb looked behind him. The blow-torch had already burned a shape the size of a doorway. He pressed against his earpiece. "They've nearly busted through."

The door of steel got kicked forward and it hit the ground with a loud *clang*. The Crimson foot soldiers spilled into the place. With too far to travel to get back to Sparks and the others in the ship, Seb said, "They're in. You go; I'll catch up."

The soldiers who'd made it into the hangar sent a volley of blaster fire at the ship, which wobbled and shook from the attack. "We're not going anywhere without you," Sparks screamed into the earpiece.

"You have to," Seb said. "I'm not running across the hangar to get to you." And with that, he ran out of the way to hide beneath one of the Crimson fleet's ships.

"I said we won't go without you," Sparks called again.

The *whoosh* of a plasma rocket shot through the hangar and scored a direct hit on the back of Sparks' ship. Another one rushed through a second later and narrowly missed, exploding into the wall and filling the air with the thick smell of smoke.

"You'll all die if you don't leave now," Seb said. "I'll find a way out of here." As he spoke, he climbed into the ship he'd hidden beneath.

A third *whoosh* and Sparks shifted her ship to the side to avoid another rocket. "Damn it," she called through the earpiece and she flew out of the hangar.

Once outside, Sparks turned her ship around so she faced back in and shouted, "I've trusted you to get out of there, Seb. Don't let me down."

"Don't let *you* down?" Seb replied as he sat in the cockpit of the ship he'd climbed into. "I'm more concerned about not letting myself down at the moment." He flicked the ignition switch and his ship shook as it sprang to life.

"Are you okay flying that thing?" Sparks said in Seb's ear.

"I'm going to have to be." He grabbed one of the handles and he lurched to the side, knocking over several drawers full of tools and crashing into a stationary ship with a loud *bang*. The shock of the crash snapped through the vessel and jolted Seb's frame. When he pulled the lever the other way, he rushed at one of the solid metal walls, but he managed to stop just before he smashed into it. One crash he could get away with, two and he wouldn't be flying out of there.

The sound of blaster fire hit the side of Seb's ship, but the shields dampened them. He glanced behind to see three of the Crimson foot soldiers, all with rocket launchers pointed his way. Just before they could fire, he pushed forward on the flight stick and shot toward the hangar's exit. Three loud explosions hit the wall just where he'd been only seconds before.

Totally out of control, Seb closed his eyes as he shot away from the hangar. When he opened them again, he found himself outside and on a collision course with Sparks.

The small Thrystian screamed as he hurtled toward them and Seb screamed louder in return.

CHAPTER 55

Fortunately Sparks had the presence of mind to pull her ship to the side at the last minute and Seb flew straight past them, yelling as he came dangerously close to a collision. Sweat made his palms damp against the flight stick and his breathing sped up, but when he looked at the open sky now before him, he relaxed a little.

A look behind at Sparks and although he saw her ship, he also saw seven ships of the Crimson fleet exit the hangar after them. The earpiece Sparks had given him seemed to stop working because he called her name into it several times and received no reply.

A few seconds later the beautiful face of SA popped up on the console in front of him. Sparks spoke. "How are you doing, Seb?"

"I'm still in the sky."

"That's good. I have some bad news for you."

"Worse than the fact that we're outnumbered in a dogfight and it's all I can do to stop myself from crashing?"

Seb physically deflated when Sparks said, "Yep. It turns out the rocket that hit us disabled our blasters."

The reality of their situation seemed slightly beyond Seb's grasp. "Wait a minute. So that means—"

"We have *no* blasters. You're on your own in this battle."

Seb looked over his shoulder again at the seven ships that had followed them out. The action of turning around made him send his ship tearing across the sky to his right. Totally out of control, Seb yanked the flight stick the other way and somehow managed to stop.

Deep breaths did nothing to slow his world down. Like in the simulators, his gift didn't work here.

"The best thing to do is follow us and keep our tail clear," Sparks said.

"I can't even see you, Sparks, let alone fly in a straight enough line to follow you." A gentle nudge on the flight stick and he turned his ship until he saw them. A nudge of the stick forward and he took off in their direction.

As Seb hurtled through the air, Sparks screamed at him, "Slow down, Seb."

Seb pulled back on the stick and the ship shot straight up. A vertical ascent, he only saw stars.

"Come on, you can do it."

"I can't, I really can't."

"Seb!" Gurt screamed through the radio. "You need to sort it out. We're going to die if you don't."

Seb closed his eyes for just a couple of seconds and tried to find the place where everything moved slowly for him. Upon opening his eyes again, he still hadn't reached it. Sweat dampened his brow and his heart raced. A look at the console and he saw SA's concerned face staring at him. A strange calm settled over him. Unlike Gurt, who spoke to him with contempt, and Sparks, who spoke to him with fear, SA looked at him like she genuinely believed in him.

For the briefest moment, Seb stared back at her before he

swallowed a warm gulp of air and relaxed his vice-like grip on the stick. The ship calmed down a little and he managed to level it out. Life still moved at the same hectic pace, but he'd bought himself some thinking time with his greater control.

When Seb turned his ship around, he saw Sparks and her getaway. The Crimson fleet closed down on her. A gentle tip of the flight stick and he dove down toward them.

The flight stick had a red trigger on it. Seb pointed the front of his vessel at the lead ship in the Crimson fleet and squeezed it. Green blaster fire rushed away from him and he felt every shot through the stick as the ship bucked. Every blast went painfully wide.

"Come on, Seb," Sparks called at him.

A slight adjustment in his course and Seb pulled the trigger again. Two of the four shots hit the lead Crimson fleet ship, cutting straight through its shield and turning the shiny silver vessel into a bright ball of flames.

"Wooooooooot!" Sparks shouted through the radio. She screamed so loud it distorted through the speakers in Seb's cockpit.

Everything moved fast, much faster than Seb had grown used to during combat, but he managed to send three more shots out and take down two of the remaining six ships. Still slightly out of control, he flew straight on a collision course with one of the Crimson fleet. The pilot had the good sense to get out of his way, saving both of them from a crash.

A sharp turn, so abrupt Seb could have sworn he heard his brain rattle, and he faced the fleet again. Several more shots and three of the four blew up in front of him.

"I thought you couldn't shoot?" Gurt called to Seb through the radio.

"I couldn't," Seb replied. "Looks like I just learned how."

Although Seb got on the back of the last ship in the fleet,

he couldn't shoot at it. Sparks sat directly in front of it. If he missed, his friends would melt in a hot explosion like the Crimson fleet had. A tilt forward on the flight stick and he sped up as he rushed towards his friends and the final enemy ship. When he saw the front of the fleet's ship glow green, he shouted at the radio, "It's charging up a shot."

"I can't do anything to get it off my tail," Sparks replied.

Seb tilted the flight stick even farther forward and sped up.

The green glow on the front of the Crimson fleet's ship burned so brightly it nearly dazzled Seb. He forced his ship into a dive before he yanked the stick back, flipping his nose up at the base of the enemy's vessel. A squeeze of the trigger and he sent two green blaster shots toward his target. Both hit, and the ship exploded into a ball of flames like all of the others had.

"We did it!" Seb yelled as he watched the pieces from the lead ship fall from the sky.

"*You* did it," Sparks replied.

"Why didn't that ship on your tail just fire their blasters?"

"You have to be much more accurate with blasters," Sparks said. "They wanted to make sure so they charged a cannon pulse. If they'd have gotten that shot off, it would have hit us without fail and we'd be dead. You saved us, Seb."

A wide smile stretched Seb's face and he looked at SA staring back at him from the screen. He then looked out of the window into space and an image of his mother flashed through his mind. Something had unlocked in him at that moment. He could fly a ship where he previously had no clue. The lunatic in the sewers came back to him. His mother had given him something special and it felt like he had much more to come.

CHAPTER 56

Although SA's face had been on the screen in Seb's console for the entirety of the dogfight, Sparks now popped up and beamed a grin at him. "You did it, Seb! You did it."

Out of breath from both the exertion of flying and the panic that he would watch his friends die in front of him, Seb caught Sparks' infectious smile and grinned back. "I did it."

Sparks leaned close to the screen and whispered, "And did your *ability* kick in?"

Seb's smile broadened. "No. I did it all at high speed."

When Sparks' tiny jaw fell loose, Seb laughed again. "Well done," she said. "Well done."

The small face of Seb's friend disappeared to be replaced by Gurt. A stern look on his face, Gurt pushed his bulbous chin forward, his broken horns prominent on the screen. He then dipped a nod. "I suppose you've got some use after all."

Whether he meant it as a joke or not, Seb laughed anyway as Gurt walked away.

SA's face popped up. The brilliance of her gaze pulled the

air from Seb's lungs, and for the first time since he'd gotten in the ship, time slowed down. It seemed like his ability kicked in to make the most of the moment.

After she'd stared at him for what simultaneously felt like forever and an instant, SA blinked slowly and smiled.

Seb's body rippled with gooseflesh and a lump lifted into his throat. He had no words as he looked back at her.

Still in shock when Sparks appeared on the screen again, Seb listened to her instructions.

"We need to get out of here. We're going to make the jump to warp speed in a minute and we can drag you through with us. I'm going to connect you to our ship now. See you on the other side, yeah?"

Still having a dry throat from his interaction with SA, Seb nodded at Sparks.

They remained connected to one another, so although Seb couldn't see Sparks, he heard her. "Right, everyone, sit down and get ready. Jumping to warp speed in five … four … three …"

On three, Gurt appeared on the screen. He'd taken SA's spot in the co-pilot's seat.

"Two …"

Gurt winked at Seb, a smug look on his fat face. He then reached forward as if to press a button on the console in front of him.

The screen suddenly went black. Seb stared at it for a second or two longer before he looked up through his windshield. The boosters on the back of Sparks' ship with George Camoron and the rest of his team glowed so brightly they left flashing lights in his eyes.

The ship then shot away from him, the large vessel quickly turning into a dot on the horizon. It didn't drag Seb with it. With the darkness of space in front of him and the planet of Solsans behind, he looked back down at the screen that had shown him the others in their ship.

It remained black.

CHAPTER 57

Alarms blared, lights flashed, the ship shook, and Seb couldn't do anything to slow it down. He might have learned how to fly a ship and shoot from one, but he hadn't mastered the art of landing yet. As the forest came into view, he pulled his seatbelt on and let go of the flight stick.

The tops of the trees slapped against the bottom of the ship, dragging their branches along its metal body with a screeching sound. A second later Seb hit a more solid part of a tree, which spun the ship out of control through the densely packed forest. Several loud bangs shook the vessel before he hit the ground.

The heavy shock of the crash landing left Seb's ears ringing and his head spun. A headache stretched from his forehead from where he'd head-butted the dashboard, and his body felt as if his skeleton had been taken apart and put back together with a piece missing.

Once Seb had unclipped from the seat, he stood up and nearly fell over again. A deep throb ran from his collarbone all the way across the front of his chest from where the seatbelt had taken the bulk of the impact. He winced at the pain and drew deep breaths.

The ship leaned at an angle because the right side of it had planted into the soft ground. Seb had to hold on to his seat to remain upright.

The screen that had linked Seb to the other ship had been shattered in the crash, but the light on the speaker beneath it still blinked. A crackle and Gurt's voice came through. "I did as you said."

"Thank you," Seb replied as he tried to blink his dizziness away.

"The others weren't too happy, but I told them it was your wish to return. That you wanted to go back for the Crimson Countess, but you didn't want to jeopardise our mission. Or put any of us in danger. Especially SA."

Seb's voice went shrill. "You said that?"

"Am I wrong?"

Seb ignored his question. "Make sure you get that rich idiot back to his daddy, and then enjoy your rest."

"We're dropping him off and coming straight back. We've already agreed on it. You can detach the speaker we're using now. We can stay in touch so we can find you again."

"No."

"No?"

"Yep. No."

"What do you mean no?" Gurt said.

"I want to do this on my own. It'll be dangerous and I don't want you all risking your lives. *I'm* the one who wants to make sure the Crimson Countess dies."

"I'm afraid you don't get to make that choice. I wasn't happy about cutting you loose like I did, and the others certainly weren't happy with me. The only way I can square it is if I come back and help."

Seb paused for a moment before he said, "Sorry, I'm going alone on this one."

Pouches hung from each arm on the pilot's seat. Each pouch contained a blaster. Seb removed one of them, aimed it at the radio and pulled the trigger.

The blaster kicked in his grip and an explosion of light and electrics filled the cockpit. A few fizzes and pops and Seb ruffled his nose at the smell of burning plastic.

The smoke cleared and Gurt's voice came through the radio again. "You missed, didn't you?"

A frown darkened Seb's view of the console in front of him and he pulled the trigger again.

This time the radio—rather than the console it sat embedded in—exploded in a shower of sparks, silencing Gurt and leaving Seb as he wished to be, well and truly on his own.

Seb stood up, slipped the blaster he'd used to shoot the console into his back pocket, and stumbled out of the ship.

Surrounded by fog in the dark forest, Seb turned around to look at the path he'd ploughed with his crash landing. A gap had been torn through the trees, the smell of sap and evergreen needles rich in the air. A large trench ran through the soft ground from where the ship had touched down.

Seb then turned back and faced the slum and elevated city of Caloon. The Crimson Countess would regret ever coming to his attention.

Aches sat in every muscle in Seb's body and he dragged a deep breath in through his clenched teeth. But the pains would pass, and one way or another, the Countess would pay for everything she'd done.

END OF BOOK TWO.

~

Thank you for reading The First Mission - Book Two of
The Shadow Order.

The Crimson War - Book Three of The Shadow Order - is
available NOW.

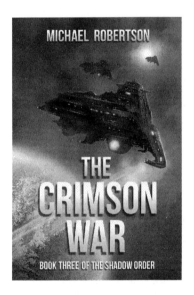

~

Would you like to be notified of all my future releases and
special offers? Join my spam-free mailing list for all of my
updates at www.michaelrobertson.co.uk

~

Want more of the Shadow Order? Reyes becomes an
important member of the Shadow Order from book five

onwards. Get to know her in - 120-Seconds: A Shadow Order Story - available NOW.

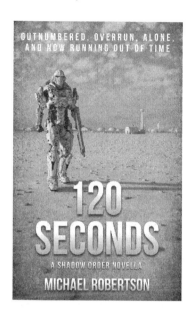

Support the Author

DEAR READER, AS AN INDEPENDENT AUTHOR I DON'T HAVE the resources of a huge publisher. If you like my work and would like to see more from me in the future, there are two things you can do to help: leaving a review, and a word-of-mouth referral.

Releasing a book takes many hours and hundreds of dollars. I love to write, and would love to continue to do so. All I ask is that you leave an Amazon review. It shows other readers that you've enjoyed the book and will encourage them to give it a try too. The review can be just one sentence, or as long as you like.

If you've enjoyed The Shadow Order, you may also enjoy my post-apocalyptic series - The Alpha Plague - Book 1 is FREE NOW.

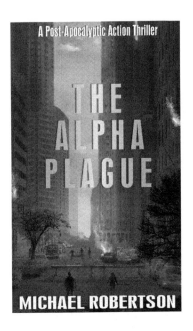

ABOUT THE AUTHOR

Like most children born in the seventies, Michael grew up with Star Wars in his life. An obsessive watcher of the films, and an avid reader from an early age, he found himself taken over with stories whenever he let his mind wander.

Those stories had to come out.

He hopes you enjoy reading his books as much as he does writing them.

Michael loves to travel when he can. He has a young family, who are his world, and when he's not reading, he enjoys walking so he can dream up more stories.

Contact
www.michaelrobertson.co.uk
subscribers@michaelrobertson.co.uk

New Reality: Truth

New Reality 2: Justice

New Reality 3: Fear

Sixth Cycle

Nuclear war has destroyed human civilization.

Captain Jake Phillips wakes into a dangerous new world, where he finds the remaining fragments of the population living in a series of strongholds, connected across the country. Uneasy alliances have maintained their safety, but things are about to change. -- Discovery **leads to danger.** -- Skye Reed, a tracker from the Omega stronghold, uncovers a threat that could spell the end for their fragile society. With friends and enemies revealing truths about the past, she will need to decide who to trust. -- Sixth **Cycle** is a gritty post-apocalyptic story of survival and adventure.

Darren Wearmouth ~ Carl Sinclair

DEAD ISLAND: Operation Zulu

Ten years after the world was nearly brought to its knees by a zombie Armageddon, there is a race for the antidote! On a remote Caribbean island, surrounded by a horde of hungry living dead, a team of American and Australian commandos must rescue the Antidotes' scientist. Filled with zombies, guns, Russian bad guys, shady government types, serial killers and elevator muzak. Dead Island is an action packed blood soaked horror adventure.

Allen Gamboa

Invasion Of The Dead Series

This is the first book in a series of nine, about an ordinary bunch of friends, and their plight to survive an apocalypse in Australia. -- Deep beneath defense headquarters in the Australian Capital Territory, the last ranking Army chief and a brilliant scientist struggle with answers to the collapse of the world, and the aftermath of an unprecedented virus. Is it a natural mutation, or does the infection contain -- more sinister roots? -- One hundred and fifty miles away, five friends returning from a month-long camping trip slowly discover that death has swept through the country. What greets them in a gradual revelation is an enemy beyond compare. -- Armed with dwindling ammunition, the friends must overcome their disagreements, utilize their individual skills, and face unimaginable horrors as they battle to reach their hometown...

Owen Ballie

~

Whiskey Tango Foxtrot

Alone in a foreign land. The radio goes quiet while on convoy in Afghanistan, a lost patrol alone in the desert. With his unit and his home base destroyed, Staff Sergeant Brad Thompson suddenly finds himself isolated and in command of a small group of men trying to survive in the Afghan wasteland. **Every turn leads to danger**

The local population has been afflicted with an illness that turns them into rabid animals. They pursue him and his men at every corner and stop. Struggling to hold his team together and unite survivors, he must fight and evade his way to safety. **A fast paced zombie war story like no other.**

W.J. Lundy

Zombie Rush

New to the Hot Springs PD Lisa Reynolds was not all that welcomed by her coworkers especially those who were passed over for the position. It didn't matter, her thirty days probation ended on the same day of the Z-poc's arrival. Overnight the world goes from bad to worse as thousands die in the initial onslaught. National Guard and regular military unit deployed the day before to the north leaves the city in mayhem. All directions lead to death until one unlikely candidate steps forward with a plan. A plan that became an avalanche raging down the mountain culminating in the salvation or destruction of them all.

Joseph Hansen

The Gathering Horde

The most ambitious terrorist plot ever undertaken is about to be put into motion, releasing an unstoppable force against humanity. Ordinary people – A group of students celebrating the end of the semester, suburban and rural families – are about to themselves in the center of something that threatens the survival of the human species. As they battle the dead – and the living – it's going to take every bit of skill, knowledge and luck for them to survive in Zed's World.

Rich Baker

Made in the USA
Columbia, SC
19 June 2021